THE TROPHY WIVES CLUB

ALI SPOONER

THE TROPHY WIVES CLUB

ALI SPOONER

Affinity
Rainbow Publications

2019

Acknowledgments

I would like to thank my fans for following my stories, providing great feedback, and encouragement. Writing wouldn't be so much fun without you. Thanks to Affinity, Irish Dragon for the cover art and the team of editors, readers, and publishers who continue to help me grow as a writer.

DEDICATION

For Rhonda. Thanks for allowing me the time to create and your support of my writing.
Love you Babes!

TABLE OF CONTENTS

CHAPTER ONE

Marley Jacobs had finished the back portion of Mrs. Melinda "Lindy" Freemont's session and was ready to finish up. "If you'll turn over, I'll finish your massage."

Marley waited until Lindy turned and filled her hands with the warmed oil. She allowed Lindy to get settled and began massaging the muscles across Lindy's chest.

"How long have you been giving me massages now?"

"I would guess a little over a year now, twice a week," Marley responded as she caressed the tense muscles with strong hands.

Lindy kept her eyes closed as she continued her questioning. "I would suspect that you actually get very little of what the center charges for the massages too."

"They call it overhead," Marley chuckled. "I've looked into opening my own spot, but the overhead really is a killer and I don't have the upfront money for that kind of investment."

Marley watched as Lindy's mouth turned up in a smile, listening to her response. "How much do they pay you here?"

Marley cocked her head at Mrs. Freemont. She usually wasn't this full of chatter. "That's kind of personal, but I gross thirty thousand."

"I'm sorry to be prying, but I do have a reasonable cause for it."

Marley chuckled softly. "That would be what, Mrs. Freemont?"

"A business opportunity, Marley, but not one that can be discussed here. Would you consider having dinner with me tonight to discuss the proposal?"

Mrs. Freemont had stirred her curiosity, but she also did not want to get her hopes up only to have it crushed. *What the hell, all I have to lose is a bit more of my pride and this place was eating it up on a regular basis.* "Sure, why not, never hurts to listen. I will be off at five."

"Do you know where Victor's is?"

"Yes, I do." Victor's was an extremely expensive steakhouse on the fringe of Northwest Atlanta. She knew where it was, but the menu was way out of her price range.

"Will you meet me there at six-thirty?"

"I can do that," Marley replied as her hands stroked down the front of Lindy's body.

Lindy was a forty something wife of the Honorable Judge, Jay W. "Dubyah" Freemont, who was at least twenty years her senior. Jay Dub, as he was most commonly referred to, was a Federal Judge who, according to his wife, was spending more time at his Washington post than at his Atlanta home.

Marley concentrated on her movements, but could not overlook the rock-hard nipples on the perfectly shaped breasts her hands had just caressed on their way down Lindy's body. This wasn't an uncommon response for most of her clientele, but was a first for Lindy. She shook the image from in front of her mind and was thankful Lindy's eyes were closed so she didn't see the flush on her cheeks.

"If I haven't told you lately young woman, you have the most marvelous hands," Lindy softly whispered, adding to the coloring of Marley's cheeks.

"Thank you, Mrs. Freemont," she managed to say after pushing the lump in her throat away.

"I have had many massages over the years, and none left me feeling the way yours do."

"Careful now or you will give me a big head," Marley chuckled, as her hands worked down Lindy's right thigh.

"I am being very sincere." Lindy propped up on her elbows and looked at, Marley. Her blue eyes were sparkling.

"Thanks, but you need to lay back now so I can finish."

Lindy smiled and complied with her request, much to Marley's relief. Her blue eyes remained locked on Marley as she concentrated on her task and she could feel her eyes giving her a close inspection. She tried her best to ignore the soft moans coming from Lindy as she deeply massaged her legs and finished up with her feet. When done, she covered Lindy's body with a cool sheet.

"All good for today. Take your time getting dressed and I will see you at six thirty Mrs. Freemont." Marley smiled at her then left the room to allow her customer to get dressed.

Marley closed the door softly behind her and walked to the small office break room to wash her hands and take a long drink of cool water. She carried a fresh bottle of water to her cubical and was making case notes when Lindy walked by. She looked up from her notes to a smile and wave as she passed. She returned the smile and turned back to her appointment book. Only one more appointment for today and then she would go home to shower before meeting with Lindy. She did a mental review of her closet in search of something decent to wear to her meeting as she waited for her next client.

After her last appointment, Marley washed up and closed down her laptop before walking out to her car for the short ride home. It was Friday night, and the rush hour traffic was brutal as usual, but Marley had found a short cut and quickly exited the interstate. Her thoughts were preoccupied, pondering Lindy's proposal and she nearly missed the turn into her apartment.

CHAPTER TWO

Marley headed straight for the shower when she opened the door to her small apartment. For a moment, she regretted agreeing to a dinner meeting with Lindy, preferring instead to spend her Friday night winding down with a few cold beers at her favorite local pub. But she had agreed and it wouldn't hurt to hear what her client was proposing over a fabulous steak dinner. Afterward, she would go for those beers, she promised herself.

Time was passing quickly as she undressed for the second time and tried on a third outfit. "This will have to do," she told herself as she slipped a light sweater over her head. She finished dressing and went to the bathroom for a spray of perfume and to run a brush through her hair. A look in the mirror told her she was presentable and actually looked pretty damned good. With a smile at the image looking back at her she grabbed her keys and walked out the door.

She arrived at Victor's at six twenty-five and found a parking spot. They had not discussed where they would meet, so she walked into the restaurant and was greeted immediately by the host.

"Ms. Jacobs?" he asked.

"Yes."

"Follow me please, Mrs. Freemont has already arrived."

Marley followed the young man through the restaurant to a small private area where Lindy was already waiting. The host pulled out a chair for Marley and left them once she was settled.

"You look very nice," Lindy remarked as Marley took her seat.

"Thanks. You look marvelous as usual."

"Flattery will get you everywhere," Lindy smiled. "Would you care for some wine?"

"Yes, thank you," Lindy poured a glass and handed it to her.

"I appreciate you meeting with me tonight, Marley."

"I have to admit, you have my curiosity piqued."

Lindy rewarded her with a charming smile. "That is good, I was hoping I would. I need to ask some personal questions before we go much further."

"Ask away," Marley lifted her wine glass to her lips.

"You have been giving me massages for over a year now and we have never discussed your personal life. I am assuming quite a lot here, but I must ask if you are a lesbian?"

Marley was very glad she had waited to take a sip of the wine until after the question. She calmly took a sip and then placed her glass on the table. "I will have faith that this is a reasonable question to be asked, but yes, I am a lesbian."

"Trust me when I say there is a perfectly good reason for the question."

A waiter arrived to take their orders and then left them again to their privacy.

"What does my sexual orientation have to do with your proposal?"

"I promise it has everything to do with it but let me explain."

"Yes, please do," Marley was trying not to sound offended.

The waiter approached with salads and bread. When he left, Lindy continued. "I have been mulling over a business venture for several months, but your participation is extremely important to me."

Marley picked up her fork and started on her salad. "I'm listening."

"I assume that you know who my husband is?"

"Yes, a very ambitious Federal Judge," Marley answered.

Lindy chuckled at her response. "Ambitious would be a good description of, Jay Dub. Anyhow, I know that he has been spending a great deal of time in DC and there have been several young women he has been spending considerable time and money on, if you catch my drift."

"He's having affairs, is that what you are saying?"

"When good old Jay Dub manages to get home, all I get from him on a rare occasion is ten humps and a slump. He takes his pleasure and quickly falls off to sleep and even that has been fairly non-existent these last few months."

Marley nearly choked on her salad when Lindy described her husband's lack of performance and decided to place her fork on her plate. She had no idea that their conversation would be taking this type of turn.

"Please continue," she said with a smirk.

"We can wait until after we eat if you would prefer," Lindy offered.

"No, I'm good," Marley picked up her fork.

"Most people would assume with the age difference that Jay Dub took me in as a trophy wife but I have my own career, my own money, so I don't depend on him for handouts." Lindy stabbed her fork into her salad. "I love him dearly and can look past his behavior. Divorce is totally out of the question, so where does that leave me?"

"Sexually frustrated," Marley said. "Sorry to be blunt."

"That is exactly where it leaves me, and I prefer your directness."

Marley cocked her head. "So, if divorce is out of the question, what do you see as your options?"

"That is where you come into the picture. Do you have a partner?"

"No, at the moment I am single, but why does that matter?"

"Would I be someone you could feel attracted to in a sexual manner?"

"You are a beautiful woman, but also a very married one," Marley answered.

Lindy smiled at her and waited for the next comment.

"I will admit if approached by you, I probably wouldn't turn away, Mrs. Freemont, if that is what you are asking."

"Please, call me Lindy and yes, that was exactly what I was asking."

The waiter arrived with their steaks. "Eat, these are too good to waste and then we will continue."

Lindy was correct, the steak was incredible. Marley pondered what she had heard so far as she enjoyed the plentiful meal. She thought she had some idea where Lindy was heading, but did not want to assume anything.

After the meal, Lindy looked across the table at her. "May I take you someplace? I have something I want you to see that may help make more sense of the conversation we are about to have."

"You have me curious, and I don't have solid plans for tonight, so I guess I'm all yours."

Lindy smiled at her eagerness. "Let's go. You can ride with me and I'll bring you back later for your car." She placed cash on the table and stood to lead Marley from the restaurant. They walked to a small sports car and Lindy unlocked the doors. They climbed inside and she started the powerful engine and drove out of the parking lot as darkness fell on Atlanta.

†

Fifteen minutes later, they pulled up in front of a large building. Lindy used her keys, opened a door and stepped inside. She flipped on a switch and the area lit up.

"What is this place?" Marley asked as they started toward a small flight of stairs.

"It is an investment piece that I have been remodeling. It used to be a small factory, but I have begun converting it to small flats. I had visions of using it as a rental property, but my vision has changed."

The room they walked through was open, nearly two thousand square feet of space, enough to create a variety of rooms. The building was much larger from the inside as they climbed the stairs and took a tour of the five flats that had already been converted to private living spaces. They were decorated with the finest of furnishings and Marley felt they could bring a fortune as rental properties.

"These are beautiful," she said as they wandered from room to room. She looked out a window and beneath the soft glow of security lights, saw a freshly surfaced tennis court waiting for players. "So, what are your plans?"

"Sit with me and I'll tell you," Lindy ushered her to a small love seat in one of the flats.

"I want some of that sumpin' sumpin' Jay Dub's been getting on the side. What's good for the goose…, but I have a plan for a very discreet operation."

"Why not just go out and get some from any of the young studs that would so easily follow you home?"

"It's not a young stud I want, besides there is the risk of accidental pregnancy and STD's. They usually have no sense of discretion either," she added as an afterthought.

"That makes sense. I can imagine how difficult it could be if it were spread around your social circle that you are getting busy with a young man."

"Speaking of social circles," Lindy said. "I have a large one as you can imagine, and many of these women are in the same boat I'm in."

"So, we have a large group of Atlanta's Elite with raging hormones?" Marley teased.

Lindy broke out in laughter. "That is one way of putting it, but I prefer to think of us as women with needs and plenty of money to meet those needs."

"So, how do I fit in this picture?" Marley turned toward Lindy.

"I thought you would never ask," Lindy looked Marley in the eyes. "I would like to convert this place into a very exclusive club, and I would like you to be the manager."

"What kind of club?"

"First, and foremost, it would be a health club complete with fitness trainers, tennis pro, massage therapists and a juice and coffee bar. The men have their "Boys' Clubs" and I want to create a strictly female environment for my friends and I to enjoy."

"I sense there is more based on our previous conversation."

"You are a sharp one, Marley." Lindy moved closer to her and placed a hand on her thigh. "In addition to a good workout, my friends and I would like some extra attention."

"Pardon my crudeness, but a whorehouse?" Marley asked.

"I would not consider the employees here as whores and I find the term completely demeaning. I envision the staff here to be well educated in their skills and willing to provide the extra care to the clientele if they so desire. Their participation is strictly voluntary, and would be well compensated above and beyond their normal salaries, always on a cash basis."

Marley sat back on the love seat as the information began to sink in.

"I am assuming with your contacts that you could staff the club with some of your friends and associates. I'm sure you aren't the only professional out there that is being taken advantage of by their employers."

Lindy's words struck a chord deep within her. She had been making the same salary since starting at the clinic five years ago and had been turned down every time she requested an increase. Still, no matter what Lindy chose to call it, it would be prostitution, then again wasn't working for anyone for money a source of that?

"I know some women who just might be interested. What kind of salaries are we talking about?"

"Yours would be eighty. The rest I will decide upon your advisement."

"Eighty thousand?" Marley nearly choked with excitement.

"Yes, and one of the flats if you want to live rent free," Lindy added. "I can easily have one built for you with a private entrance."

"Walk me through the rest of the building and tell me what you have planned."

Lindy smiled and they left the flat to walk through the rest of the top floor. There was room for several more flats and when they reached the end of the hallway there was one large room, with several windows and a skylight. "I thought this would be perfect for you."

Marley's eyes lit up at the size of the room, easily three times the size of her apartment. There was a small kitchen, but she didn't spend much time in the kitchen and the bathroom was decked out with a whirlpool tub and separate shower.

"There are no drugs or other illegal activities in this plan are there?"

"No, of course not, the main business is the health spa and the upstairs activities…well they are bonus opportunities for the staff."

"You have friends who are interested in this venture?"

"I have checks for $20,000 each from twenty-five women who are very interested in this project."

"That's half a million dollars," Marley let out a low whistle.

"Twenty thousand dollars for a health club membership and discretion is nothing for these women," Lindy said.

They started walking down a staircase to the bottom floor. "I thought we would turn this into the fitness area, with massage rooms along the back wall, a set of showers and a locker room over there and maybe even a Roman bath."

Marley was deep in thought as they finished the tour of the building. When she first decided to become a massage therapist, she took a lot of teasing from her friends about wanting to work in a massage parlor. Marley was quick to explain to them that her role as a therapist was to help the body relax and heal itself and there was nothing sexual about her skills. Had she been deceiving herself in believing that and would she be crossing that barrier by taking this position?

Lindy walked slowly, allowing Marley an opportunity to digest the information. "After the construction is complete, there will be no men allowed inside the property. This will be an all-woman haven, so you will need to hire someone handy with tools to be on call for any problems." When they returned to the front area Lindy said, "This will be the main entrance. I think this would make for a great social area, a juice bar and coffee station."

Marley's head was swimming with ideas.

"So, what do you think so far?"

"I think you have a great plan in place."

"Oh, you will have an office in the back corner and there will be an area for laundry equipment as well."

"I have to admit this sounds almost too good to be true, but I'm a massage therapist and I have no idea how to run a business."

"That part I can teach you. Once the equipment is set up and staff is on board, you will see the business will take care of itself."

"When do you hope to open for business?"

"The building remodel will be complete in two weeks. I was hoping we could have a fitness expert on board with us next week to select and order the equipment she will need. Once that is in, the rest should be relatively easy, so roughly a month from now."

"I have to give a two week notice at the clinic."

Lindy chuckled. "Say yes, and you will be on the payroll starting tomorrow. I respect your intention to work out a notice and think we could accomplish what we need to after you get off work."

Marley turned to Lindy, her eyes sparkling with excitement. "Yes, let's give this a shot."

Lindy pulled her into an embrace. "You will be glad you did, I promise," she said as she hugged her.

Marley's eyes fell to Lindy's lips as she remained in her arms and she saw Lindy's tongue snake across to wet them. She leaned forward and let her lips brush across them in a soft kiss.

Lindy was flushed when she broke the kiss. "I should probably test out your skills now that you are my newest employee," she said with a coy smile.

Marley returned her smile and took her by the hand and led her back upstairs to the first flat. Two hours later, Lindy rested her head on Marley's shoulder. "That was better than I have been imagining for almost a year now," she said with a contented smile. "If all the staff is as talented as you, we will have a very successful business."

"What do you plan to call this place?" Marley asked as her hand stroked down Lindy's back.

"The TWC."

"Which stands for?"

"The Trophy Wives Club," Lindy said.

Marley chuckled. "I love it."

"Will you meet me here tomorrow to start making some plans on the staffing portion of the project?"

"Sure, just let me know what time."

"How about ten? I'll treat you to lunch once we have finished," Lindy stood to begin dressing.

"That sounds great to me."

✝

Lindy drove Marley back to the restaurant to retrieve her car. "I will see you tomorrow," she said and stepped out into the night.

She watched Lindy drive off and slipped behind the wheel of her car. The clock on her dash read 11:30 and she decided to stop by the pub for a cold beer before heading home.

When she pulled into the lot at the pub, she smiled to see a black Harley parked on the sidewalk. The bike belonged to Luna Wolf, a full-blooded Cherokee woman who was the epitome of a chiseled female body. She also had the reputation as a player who loved to please women. It was also Marley's good fortune that Luna was a certified personal trainer who worked at a local gym. She would be a perfect pick for the TWC fitness trainer. As she walked in the pub her eyes were immediately drawn to the dance floor where Luna was seducing a striking blonde. Marley smiled back at her and walked to the bar for an ice-cold beer.

She sat at the bar and when the song ended, she looked into the mirror behind the counter to see the leather clad Luna approaching her. She lowered the beer to the bar as Luna slipped her arms around her from behind. "Where have you been?" she asked.

"Here and there, but working mostly. How are you doing Luna?"

"I'm doing great thanks," she slipped onto the barstool next to her. "What brings you out this time of night?"

"A cold beer to help me wind down," Marley said which was true. Finding Luna at the pub, was like hitting a jackpot.

"I could think of a few ways to help relax you," Luna purred.

15

Marley was one of the few women in the pub who didn't trip all over themselves to jump into bed with Luna.

"I'm sure you could, but I have a serious proposition for you."

"Something serious on a Friday night? You have been working too hard."

"I think it will be something you would love to be a part of. Grab a fresh drink and join me outside."

"May I have a bottle of water Terry?" Luna asked the bartender. Luna loved the bar scene for obvious reasons, but she never put an ounce of alcohol in her body.

Marley took her beer and walked with Luna out to a private grilling area and sat at a small picnic table. "Are you still a fitness trainer at the club?"

"Yeah, I'm still there." The scowl on her face gave Marley courage to proceed.

"What do you make there?"

"Thirty in a good year."

"Would you leave for forty and a potential for a lot more under the table doing what you enjoy the most?"

Luna sat her bottle of water on the table and looked across at Marley. "You look like the cat that ate the canary girl. What have you gotten yourself into?"

"Something I think you would be perfectly suited for."

"I would love to ditch the club, so tell me what you have in mind."

"I was hired tonight to start a very special, very exclusive, women's health center, and I need someone who can be a fitness trainer and can start the program from the ground up."

"Sounds interesting, but a private club can be very difficult to maintain."

"Not at twenty thousand per year membership fees," Marley said.

"Twenty thousand! Geez Louise, who has that kind of dough these days?"

"Like I said, it is very exclusive, and we have twenty-five members already paid in advance to be a part of this. You would have complete control over the equipment purchases to set up the program just the way you want."

"Complete control? No limits?"

"You can have anything you need to start the program."

"Okay, but what's the catch?"

"There will be some requests for additional services."

Luna raised an eyebrow. "What kind of services?"

"The clientele we will be serving are trophy wives that aren't getting much at home."

"You have got to be shitting me, Marley."

"Trust me, I'm not. Thirty to forty something wives of some of the most influential men in the state. The boys are getting some on the side and the wives are ready for their share. They are willing to pay the price for discreet female companionship in cash, above and beyond your normal salary."

"This isn't April first, Marley."

Marley chuckled. "I promise you I am not joking, but I am pressed for time. I have to have the club staffed and ready to open in a month."

"Are you sure this isn't just some ploy to start a fancy massage parlor for the horny rich couples?"

"Men are off limits once the construction is complete, and the health spa is the main business. The extra activities are just that, and staff are no way forced into participating. It's a legitimate business that would offer great opportunities for staff and clientele."

Marley could see Luna seriously considering her options and took out a scrap of paper and jotted down an address. "Think it over tonight and if you are interested, meet me at this address at three tomorrow. Just remember, discretion is the key to this program."

"I understand. Thanks for thinking of me."

"You would be perfect and I'm sure you will have all the loving you can handle." Marley grinned at Luna. "Hey Luna?"

"Yeah Marley."

"Bring some of your toys with you tomorrow just in case the boss wants a demonstration during your interview."

"No problem at all," Luna said with a devilish grin.

Marley finished her beer and dropped the bottle in the garbage can. "Have a good night and I hope to see you tomorrow." She left Luna simmering in her thoughts. She climbed into her car and drove for home, barely finishing undressing before her exhausted body hit the bed. She was tired and excited, and that excitement brought her the most wonderful dreams.

✝

Luna watched Marley leave the club and walk to her car. She and Marley had known each other for some time, but she could never get Marley to take her flirtations seriously. They had become friends even though Luna longed for more. Marley came out to the club on occasion, but Luna never saw her leave with anyone or spend much time with anyone other than herself. *Maybe if we were to work together, Marley would realize my feelings for her were genuine. Then again, those extra services she talked about may only strengthen her reputation as a player, but Marley would also be participating in those herself, wouldn't she?*

Someone grabbing her hand, made Luna realize she'd been staring out into the darkness several minutes after

Marley left. She turned to find a young lady she had been dancing with earlier standing beside her.

"Don't be so serious, come back inside and dance with me."

"Thanks for the offer, but I'm going to call it an early night. I've got big plans for tomorrow. Maybe another time."

"I'll be waiting, Romeo," the woman sashayed back inside the club.

She waved to the bartender on her way to the front door and stepped out into a beautiful Atlanta night. Luna straddled her bike and smiled to herself when the powerful engine roared to life. She pulled out of the lot and enjoyed the feel of the cool wind as it blew against her face. When she arrived at her apartment, she pulled her baby under the covered porch and slipped quietly inside to keep from waking her friends.

CHAPTER THREE

Marley showered and dressed in slim fit jeans, a form fitting shirt and a pair of well-worn Doc Martens. She downed a bowl of cereal and brushed her teeth before starting out to meet Lindy. When she pulled into the parking lot Lindy had already arrived and was sitting at a table in the social area when she stepped inside the door. "Good morning."

"Good morning, Marley. How are you today?"

"I'm great thanks, and you?"

"Wonderful, I haven't slept that good in ages."

Marley grinned as she thought of the surprise she had planned for Lindy later in the day. After a round with Luna, Marley was certain Lindy would sleep even better tonight.

"Are you a coffee drinker?"

"Yes, I am."

"Then help yourself to a cup over at the bar," Lindy said.

Marley returned with coffee in hand and sat at the table with Lindy who reached down into a bag and pulled out an envelope. "This is for you."

Marley picked up the envelope and poured the contents into her hand. There were several keys and two one hundred-dollar bills.

"The keys are to the front door, your office door, and the door to your flat."

"And the money?" Marley asked.

"Payment for an enjoyable evening."

"I thought that was a part of the interview process," Marley grinned and pushed the bills back toward Lindy.

Lindy frowned and caught Marley's hand by the wrist. "Rule number one, you never turn down cash from a client. You earned it and were worth every penny of it. Rule number two, there are no freebies."

"Understood, but at least allow me to buy lunch today," Marley tucked the bills into her pocket.

"That I can do. Let's talk about getting your office set up and staffing the club. I have picked out some furniture I think would look good in your office, but will wait for your approval."

Marley looked at the selections Lindy had made and was pleased with her decisions. "That looks fine to me."

"We will have to go and try out some office chairs later, but I will go ahead and order the rest of the furniture. I have also ordered a computer system and network that will be installed Monday."

"That sounds wonderful. I think I may have found our fitness instructor last night. I have asked her to come and meet you at three today if she's interested."

"Fantastic news, that's the one we need to get rolling as quickly as possible to get equipment ordered, delivered and set up. Did you discuss an offer of money?"

"I suggested forty thousand as a salary," Marley said.

"Is she worth more?"

"I will leave that up to you to decide, but she is a very capable trainer. I think you will be pleased with her. If you feel we need to bump the offer, we certainly can."

"Let's see how this afternoon goes and we will discuss it later."

"Are there other rules I need to be concerned with?"

"I'm sure I will make some up as we go along," Lindy smiled.

"You're the boss." Marley grinned. "I know you have probably thought this through, but how do you plan on inspections and a possible police raid?"

"The inspections are all announced visits and we will ensure they are done prior to business hours, which by the way will be ten to six Monday through Friday."

"And a potential police raid if they get wind of the upstairs activity?"

"We are conveniently located just outside of Atlanta proper city limits, which places us in County jurisdiction. Trust me when I say the boys at County have much more important fish to fry."

"I just don't relish the thought of ending up in the Big House."

"I guarantee you won't. Even if by some odd chance you were arrested, it would just be a misdemeanor charge and with Jay Dub's connections it would quickly be dismissed. You are not listed as owner for your protection."

"I didn't think I would be an owner."

"You will definitely have a share of the profits if this takes off like I have planned," Lindy said.

Marley nodded, and returned to the task at hand. "What other staff do I need to recruit?"

"Do you think we will need another fitness trainer?"

"That probably wouldn't hurt."

"A fitness trainer, three massage therapists, a receptionist/juice bar operator/part time laundry person, and a tennis instructor," Lindy suggested.

"I have some ideas about all but the tennis instructor, but I will put some feelers out for that one"

"I think I can help you with that. There is a woman at the Country Club who I think would be perfect."

"Why don't you see if we can meet with her soon," Marley suggested.

"Is tomorrow afternoon good for you?"

"It can be."

"I will give her a call later today and see what she has planned."

"I don't know about you, but I'm starting to get hungry," Marley said. "What would you like for lunch?"

"Something sinful," Lindy said.

"The Varsity," Marley asked?

"Oh, that is perfect. Come on and I'll drive."

They returned to the club after gorging themselves on burgers and fries then continued developing their lists. Marley heard the deep rumble of Luna's bike as she arrived and looked up to Lindy. "I think our fitness trainer has just arrived."

"Well by all means let's go welcome her."

When Lindy opened the door to find Luna ready to knock, she gasped softly. Luna's black hair was pulled into a ponytail and the tank top she wore displayed her beautiful biceps and upper body. Marley could feel the heat ignite as Lindy's eyes took her in. Stifling a chuckle, she said, "Mrs. Freemont, this is Luna Wolf."

"I am so pleased to meet you," Lindy said unable to hide her southern drawl or the purr disguised in her voice.

"Likewise, Ma'am," Luna said with a charming smile.

"Please come in, Luna," Marley watched as Lindy's eyes got a good view of the tight jeans caressing the well-formed cheeks of Luna's ass. Oh yes, the heat definitely went up another notch or two she thought, as Lindy followed Luna into the room.

"Would you like some coffee?" Lindy asked.

"No thank you ma'am, I don't consume any type of stimulant. I would appreciate a bottle of water if you have one." Luna placed a small bag on the floor beside her chair.

"Sit still and I will get it," Marley left Luna and Lindy sitting at the table. "Luna, why don't you give Mrs. Freemont a rundown of your experience?"

Luna easily rattled off her career as a fitness trainer as if she were reading from an imaginary resume placed in front of her eyes.

"That sounds quite extensive," Lindy said. "Have you ever started a program from scratch?"

"No ma'am, but I know exactly what I would buy and how I would set it up."

"Would you like to see the area designated for the fitness center?" Marley asked as she handed Luna the bottle of water.

"Most definitely," Luna answered.

"Mrs. Freemont, would you like to do the honors?"

"Oh Marley, stop with the Mrs. Freemont already and just call me Lindy. You too, Luna," she rose from the table.

"Yes, Ma'am," Marley grinned.

"Follow me, and I will give you the grand tour."

Marley followed behind them as Lindy explained what each of the areas was designed for in the downstairs section.

"I could set up a premier program with all this space," Luna voice sounding dreamy.

"I assume Marley has explained the activities that will be held upstairs?"

"She assured me that upstairs would be what I would enjoy the most," Luna smirked.

"Very well then," Lindy showed the flats off to Luna who was most impressed with the décor.

"These places are beautiful," she said as they approached the stairwell to return downstairs.

They sat around the table and Lindy looked at Luna. "Does this sound like something you are interested in?"

"I would have total control over the development and implementation of the fitness program?"

"Absolutely. Marley and I would also recommend you bringing another full-time instructor on board to assist you."

"That would be awesome, and the salary is forty thousand?"

Lindy smiled at Marley who returned her smile and nodded her head.

"How about if we sweeten the pot to fifty," Lindy asked.

"Sweet Jesus, can I start tomorrow?"

"Yes, on a part time basis until you work out your notice at your present job. I would like to see a draft proposal of the equipment you would need and pricing as quickly as possible."

"I can have that ready by tomorrow. Marley said there may also be a test of other skills during the interview. Is this true?"

Lindy looked at Marley and gave her a sly smile. "Well, yes, it is Luna. I was just getting to that."

"I will continue my work down here," Marley said.

Luna rose and picked up the small bag she had brought in with her and followed Lindy up the stairs. Marley tried her best to concentrate on the list she was making but the moans of pleasure echoing down from upstairs inside the empty building made it very difficult. She finally gave up, poured herself another cup of coffee and walked outside to look at the tennis facilities. When she walked back inside, Lindy was walking downstairs with a very satisfied grin on her face, followed by Luna.

"I guess I will see you tomorrow afternoon," Luna said. "Give me a call later if you can Marley."

"Will do," Marley said as Luna softly closed the door.

Lindy was smiling down at Marley. "Girl, she rocked my world," a rush of heat flamed her face.

"I take it you approve of the selection then?"

"I don't care if she doesn't know anything about fitness, the way she moves that body was fantastic."

"Much better than ten humps and a slump?"

"Oh, my goodness yes, I think she could have gone on for hours. I can see we will need to invest in some resources for the upstairs."

Marley broke out laughing. "I think I would suggest you give each employee a budget for toys and other supplies and let them select their own. I'm sure no one would object if you selected some of your choosing either."

Lindy slumped back down to her seat with a giddy smile on her face. Marley knew she would be useless for the rest of the afternoon. "Why don't you head home and try to make contact with the tennis instructor, and I will meet you back here in the morning?"

"That sounds like a marvelous idea. Will you be heading home too?"

"I will shortly, there are a few things I would like to do."

"Okay, goodbye then," Lindy floated out the door.

"See you tomorrow Boss."

Marley took the pad of paper and drew out a rough sketch of the downstairs with each area designated, then began making a list of equipment and supplies that would need to be ordered for each of the areas. When she felt fairly certain she had a good start, she tore off the sheet of paper, and after locking the door behind her started for home.

She booted up her laptop and remembered Luna's request to call so she took out her cell and dialed Luna's number.

"Hello," Luna said.

"Hey Luna, this is Marley, what's up?"

"Pinch me so I know I'm not dreaming."

"I told you this would be something you would jump at."

"You are so right my friend, but I need some help."

"What can I do?"

"I assume you have wireless internet?"

"Yes, I do."

"I stopped off and bought a laptop, but I don't have internet access. Can I come over and use yours?"

"Only if you bring dinner," Marley teased.

"Is Chinese take-out okay with you?"

"That's perfect, I'm home now so anytime you're ready, come on over."

"Uh Marley."

"Yes Luna?"

"I need an address sweetheart."

"Yes, I guess that would help." Marley gave her the address.

"Sweet, I will see you soon," Luna ended the call.

†

Marley went to work researching equipment online and printed out a dozen or more pages of prices that she was reviewing when her doorbell rang.

Luna stood at the door, a large bag of Chinese food in one hand and a laptop in a box in the other. "Come on in," Marley said taking the bag of food. "You can take the laptop out and put it by mine while I set out the food."

"I'll be right back," Luna walked back to the car she had borrowed from one of her room mates. She returned moments later with a six pack of water, a bottle of wine and a small briefcase. "I wasn't sure what kind of wine you drank so I took a wild guess," she handed a bottle of red to Marley.

"This will do perfectly," Marley inspected the bottle before removing the cork to let the wine breathe. "You can stick those bottles in the fridge and grab us two cold ones to have with dinner."

Luna joined Marley at a small breakfast nook and took the plate she was offering. "That smells terrific. Let's see what you got." Marley began opening containers and moaned when she saw Sesame Chicken and beef stir fry loaded with vegetables. There were also egg rolls, fried rice, crab Rangoon and of course a handful of fortune cookies. "A bit hungry, were you?" she teased.

"I have no clue what you like to eat Marley, so I reviewed the menu and ordered several items."

"For being clueless, you did very well. Let's feast, my friend." Marley began passing containers.

Marley was amazed at the amount of food Luna consumed. "How do you keep your shape when you eat like that?"

"Work like a horse, eat like a horse my mama said." Luna smirked. "Being blessed with a high metabolism doesn't hurt either."

Marley reached for a fortune cookie and handed it to Luna. Luna handed her one as well. "Let's see what Confucius has in store for us today."

"Fortune smiles upon you," Luna read as Marley opened her cookie and smiled. "Well?"

"The path to your future has just begun," Marley read.

"I'd say we both have become very lucky over the past twenty-four hours. Thanks again for thinking of me."

"I can't think of anyone else I would rather be my partner in crime."

"I hope that means you will be my prison bitch if we go down for this," Luna teased.

Marley laughed, "No way, you're going to be mine."

"Are we taking a huge risk with this venture?"

"A risk yes, but I think we are well protected. I will be living in the end flat and I intend to recommend to Lindy that we set the rest of the flats up to look lived in just in case we ever have to answer questions."

"That's not a bad idea. I think some security cameras and an alarm system would be a great help as well."

"Duly noted, I think we can shore up the front entrance too, to make it more secure as well. It would at least give us a bit more time in case of a raid."

"Do you think that is very likely?"

"Not really, Lindy has thought this plan out well. The property is outside of the city limits and the County boys are terribly understaffed. As long as we remain discreet, I don't see any problems."

"I hope Lindy will screen these sugar mamas well so they don't go blabbing about their Sugar Shack. Are you worried about STD's? If these boys are dipping their wicks into other pots, are we at risk of catching anything?"

"I don't think we are at a high risk. The sex between these couples is very infrequent, and I doubt the women would risk an STD for themselves and take precautions. The husbands aren't the kind to pick someone off the streets. I think if we utilize safety precautions and good sanitation, we minimize our risks even further."

"You don't worry about them bragging to other non-members?"

"Once they get a taste of you my friend, TWC will become Atlanta's best."

"You are such a smooth talker."

"Didn't you see the smile of complete satisfaction on Lindy's face today?"

"She did look pretty content."

"Imagine twenty-five of them."

"I better have seconds then," Luna grabbed the container of fried rice.

"You go right ahead my friend," Marley walked to the kitchen for a wine glass and poured herself a glass.

"Me too," Luna said.

"What do you mean me too?" Marley raised an eyebrow in surprise. "I didn't think you ever put alcohol in that temple of a body you have."

"I rarely ever do, but this is a special occasion. We have to celebrate. Opportunities like the one we've been handed don't come often."

Marley chuckled and poured another glass of wine and carried them to the table where the laptops were set up. "When you finish feeding that beast, come over and I'll get you set up on the internet and wireless printing."

"Cool," Luna put down the rice container.

"Do you have any ideas for a second fitness instructor?"

"As a matter of fact, I do, and also for a receptionist/juice bar/laundry person."

"Good, do you think you can make contact with them in the morning and see if they are interested?"

"Yes, I will and I'm sure they will be. Any idea on salaries, if they ask?"

"I'd say forty for the fitness instructor and twenty-five for our all-around girl. That may seem high, but she won't be able to tap into the bonus system like the rest of us."

"I think that's reasonable."

"Okay Luna, let's get you set up so you can start earning your keep."

"Yes, Boss, I am at your disposal," Luna reached into her brief case for a notepad filled with lists and placed it on the table. "First though," she raised her wine glass. "To our future."

Marley picked up her glass and gently tapped it against Luna's. "To our future," she repeated and took a sip of wine. "You really did good picking this wine."

"Thanks, but I must admit I had help from a cute store clerk."

"Send her my compliments when you see her again."

They worked until almost midnight and drained a large portion of the bottle of wine. When she could no longer hold her head up, Marley looked at Luna. "I think we should call it a night and get some sleep."

"One more page to print and I think I will be all set."

Marley took a look at the near empty wine bottle and the goofy grin on Luna's face. "No driving home for you tonight."

"I'm okay to drive," Luna tried to protest.

"Oh no you are not, little Miss. I'm not a wine drinker. You are staying here tonight."

"Yes, Boss."

"You will have to sleep with me, but no hanky panky. We both need a good night's sleep."

"You take all the fun out of it. I have to warn you I can't sleep in clothes."

"That's okay, believe it or not I have seen a naked woman before."

"Lead the way then, Ma'am."

"The bedroom is straight through there. I'm going to pick up the kitchen quickly and I'll join you in just a few."

"May I help?"

"No, my kitchen is not big enough for two, but thanks for offering and for a great dinner."

"You are most welcome," Luna headed for the bedroom. She turned around and called out. "Marley"

"Yes, Luna."

Luna reached out and pulled Marley into a hug. "I just wanted to say thank you again for including me in this adventure."

"You are very welcome. I think we'll make an unstoppable team."

Luna shot her a cockeyed grin. "Yes, we will, Boss."

†

Luna walked into the bedroom. She removed her clothes and piled them beside the bed. A hug? I should have kissed the woman of my dreams. Luna chastised herself. Probably would have gotten a slap or at least a good talking to. She grinned and found she couldn't help herself. Her face was always sore from smiling so much whenever she was around Marley. Luna pulled the covers back and slipped into the cool sheets and snuggled into the pillow that smelled like Marley.

†

Marley placed the containers of leftover food in the fridge and tossed the empty containers in the trash. She rinsed their dishes, placed them in the dishwasher and replaced the cork in the bottle of wine. Her efforts only took about ten minutes, but when she entered the bedroom, she found Luna fast asleep in her bed, a sweet smile playing across her face. Marley walked into the bathroom, undressed, slipping an oversized t-shirt over her head and brushed her teeth. She turned off the light, and carefully climbed into the bed. She rested her head on the pillow and listened to the soft purring of Luna's breathing as she turned toward the sound and drifted peacefully to sleep.

CHAPTER FOUR

Marley woke once during the night to find Luna's head resting on her shoulder and her arm draped comfortably across her stomach. She smiled to herself and had to admit Luna did have a beautiful body and was tempted for a moment to stroke her hand down the smooth skin of her back. She resisted her desires and closed her eyes to drift back to sleep.

When she awoke hours later her bed was empty and she could hear Luna moving around her kitchen. She crept from the bed and walked in to find Luna in one of her t-shirts working steadily at the stove. "Something smells good." She rubbed her sleepy eyes.

Luna jumped at the sound of her voice. "Good morning, I hope I didn't wake you."

"No, it was time for the alarm to go off. What are you cooking?"

"I thought I would make us an omelet for breakfast."

"Did I have ingredients for omelets?"

"You had eggs and some cheese and a little bit of ham, so I think we're good. Would you pour us some juice?"

"I have orange and apple."

"Apple for me please."

Marley poured two large glasses of juice and placed them on the counter and went to start a pot of coffee. She was surprised and pleased to find Luna had already made a pot.

"I guessed at the number of scoops, but maybe it's drinkable," she shrugged.

"It looks and smells great," Marley poured a cup. "Not bad for a teetotaler," she teased after taking a sip.

Marley watched as Luna slid a huge omelet onto a plate and was relieved when she cut it in half and slid one half onto another plate. "Do you use hot sauce or ketchup?"

"A shot of hot sauce would be perfect," Marley said as her mouth began to water.

Luna walked to the fridge and located a bottle of hot sauce and dowsed each half with a shot of the spicy liquid. "I do believe we are ready to eat."

They carried their plates and juice over to the breakfast nook. "This is fantastic," Marley moaned when she bit into the omelet.

"I'm glad you approve, Ma'am."

"Is there anything you can't do?"

"Iron. I end up with more wrinkles than I started out with."

"That's a shame, I was about ready to propose to you," Marley said, taking another bite.

"I can take the clothes to the cleaners."

Marley smiled and kept eating.

"What time are you going to the club?" Luna asked.

"I thought I would go in about ten, why?"

"I would like to join you if I could and maybe get you to look over the proposal before Lindy shows up."

"Since you cooked breakfast, I reckon I do owe you."

"Naw, but I would appreciate your opinion."

"Not a problem," Marley looked over the rim of her coffee mug. She was stuffed and pushed the plate away. "That was really good."

"Thanks. I don't often cook."

"Well I'm glad you did this morning. That really hit the spot."

Marley loaded the dishwasher and poured another cup of coffee. "I'm going to take a shower so I can get moving."

"I will head out now and see you around ten."

"That sounds good, lock the door behind you when you leave please."

"Will do, Boss," she winked.

†

Marley took her coffee and walked into the bathroom to start the shower. For a brief second, she considered inviting Luna to shower with her, but she knew if she did the morning would be spent in bed. So instead, Marley started the water and undressed. Sleeping beside Luna and sharing breakfast certainly had her stirred up. She just shook her head and stepped under the warm water. She could think of dozens of women that would not have turned Luna away.

When she finished showering, Marley walked to her bedroom to dress. The t-shirt Luna had worn while cooking was folded and placed at the end of the made bed. She picked it up and lifted it to her face and just as she thought, the shirt smelled like Luna. It was a very pleasant smell and brought a smile to her face. She dropped it back onto the bed and finished dressing. She walked into the kitchen and saw the laptop back in the box and the briefcase sitting on the table with a note.

'Marley, will you please bring this to the club with you? I will be on my bike when I meet you later. Thanks, Luna.'

She rinsed her cup and carried the first load out to her car. Marley returned inside and picked up the stack of papers she had printed the night before and tucked them into her briefcase, then left her apartment.

When she arrived at the club, Marley saw Lindy's sports car in the lot and a truck sporting a local contractor's signage. She carried her materials into the front room and placed them on the table before going in search of Lindy. She noticed an envelope with Luna's name on it and smiled as she left the room. They were completing a walkthrough of the downstairs as she approached.

"Tom, this is Marley, she will be managing the club."

"Nice to meet you, Ma'am." He offered her his hand.

Marley gave him a firm handshake, "Nice to meet you too, Tom." She noticed he had a set of floor plans rolled up beneath his arm and she turned to Lindy. "I have a few security recommendations I would like to discuss when you have a minute."

"Go for it," Lindy said.

"I thought it may be helpful if we had a heavier front door and had the reception area secured from the rest of the building. A security door leading upstairs wouldn't be a bad idea either."

"Will that present a problem for you Tom?"

"None whatsoever. I can add them into the plans and get your approval before finalizing those two areas."

"Tom is pulling a second crew in starting this week to work on the club. We are going to add a Roman bath at the end of the massage rooms, if that's good with you."

"That sounds perfect and should make it easier to plumb."

"It will be close, but I'll do whatever you need to get this project completed by the end of the month."

"Thanks, Tom. I will be stopping in periodically the next two weeks and then Marley will be here full time to put the finishing touches on the place in preparation for our grand opening."

They walked back to the front door. "We will be on the job by seven in the morning," he promised and walked out to his truck to leave.

"I liked your suggestions for security," Lindy said.

"I also think we can put a video surveillance system and alarms in as well, but that is completely up to you." Marley nodded her head toward the stairs. "Might not be a bad idea to have a few minutes warning before we have some unwanted visitors upstairs."

"I don't think that will be a problem, but it won't hurt to have a system in place. What did the two of you come up with last night?"

"We both put together lists of equipment and supplies we will need to complete the start up. If you would like, we can start with my list and Luna should be here shortly."

†

She and Lindy took a seat at the table and began reviewing her lists. Lindy made several additions, such as linens and towels that Marley had overlooked. They heard the rumbling of Luna's bike pull into the parking lot. Lindy reached into her pocket and pulled out a credit card to hand to Marley.

"There is a one hundred-thousand-dollar line of credit on this card. I think it should be adequate to order the materials you will need."

"I will place the orders tonight," Marley said as Luna came bouncing in.

She sat down at the table with them and her eyes came to rest on the envelope. Lindy pushed it toward her and watched her eyes light up as she opened it. She poured out the set of keys, tucking them away in her pocket and slipped the envelope in her back pocket.

"Thanks," she said.

"Welcome aboard," Lindy said with a grin. "Starting tomorrow, the construction crew will be doubled so we can be ready to go by the beginning of next month. I will make plans for a grand opening event while the two of you get us staffed and operational with equipment and supplies." She turned to Luna. "I have already approved Marley's list, so let's see what you have in mind."

Luna opened her briefcase to remove her print outs and the hand drawn plan of the fitness area she designed.

"This should do quite well," Lindy said as Luna explained her plans. When she turned back to Marley, she was wearing a devilish grin. "I have arranged for you to meet with the tennis instructor at two today if that is good with you? Her name is Elin Combs."

"We will also be meeting with several other potential staff today, so hopefully we will be fully staffed soon," Marley said.

"Excellent," Lindy pulled out a small pocket calendar. "The first is a Friday. I was thinking we could have our grand opening on the afternoon of the second."

"That should be just fine," Marley said.

"One more thing," Lindy said. "Uniforms, I was thinking turquoise shorts with peach golf shirts with turquoise embroidery. What do you think?"

"I like that combination. It's very chic." Marley agreed and they looked at Luna who nodded in agreement.

"Very well, start me a list of short, shirt and shoe sizes and I will take care of the clothing," Lindy said.

"Yes ma'am, I'll take care of that," Luna said.

"Luna, I noticed the equipment vendor you selected is local. Do you think they will have most of it in stock?"

"If not, I will ask them for a rush order."

"Good, the flooring will be down in the fitness center tomorrow, and I am anxious to see the equipment installed. If you two can arrange your schedules, go first thing in the morning to order and pay for the equipment."

"That will help to let the club start taking shape," Marley said.

It was a tossup as to who was more excited as they chatted and made notes of additional assignments.

†

Lindy went out at lunch and brought them back sandwiches, then left for home. She did not want to appear overly anxious as they met with the potential new staff, especially Elin since she was the one to recommend her. She wanted Marley to form her own opinion of the young woman.

"I will be in touch with you two this week if that's okay," Lindy said as she rose to leave.

"Yes, no problem," they both answered, and Luna gave Lindy her cell number.

"Good luck this afternoon." She left the club.

†

Luna looked at Marley with a grin. "Dayum, Girlfriend."

Marley returned her mischievous smile. "What?"

"This is going to be so much fun."

"Yeah, I think so too. I'm really looking forward to getting away from the clinic."

Luna laughed. "I called the owner last night and gave him a one-week notice. He was none too pleased, but I don't care if he lets me go earlier, I can just spend more time here getting the club ready."

"I wish I could say the same. I'm sure the clinic is going to work me down to the last minute."

"At least there is an end in sight for you, my friend. When are you planning to move in?"

"I was hoping to be here by next weekend, why?"

"I'm interested in subletting your place and will help you with moving if you need some help. I have friends with trucks."

"I'm paid up through the month, but I'm sure the landlord would jump at you subletting. I will arrange it with him tonight and start packing."

"Just let me know when you need some trucks and muscle."

"Well the flat here is mostly furnished so it will be mostly clothes and some personal belongings. Do you need the furniture?"

"I will gladly buy it off you. I'm sort of starting from scratch here. The friends I share an apartment with own all the furnishings. All I really own are some clothes and my bike. It's easier to pick up and move that way."

Marley thought she heard a tone of sadness in Luna's voice. She smiled at her, "No problem, we can work out the details later." They heard a car door close and moments later a knock on the door.

Marley went to the door and found an adorable blonde woman standing there. She smiled as she reached out her hand. "I'm Marley, you must be Elin."

"Yes, I am," she returned Marley's smile.

"Please come in and I will introduce you to Luna, our fitness director, and we will give you a tour of the facilities."

She completed the introductions and they went on a tour of the club. When they had completed the downstairs tour, Luna left them to check out the tennis facilities alone.

"Lindy has done a wonderful job of planning for the club," Elin said as they walked toward the courts and small dressing room.

"Yes, she has. Did she explain about the upstairs activities or bonus program as she calls it?"

Elin let out a soft chuckle. "Yes, she did. I am already quite familiar with most of the women who will be members and I have no problem making a little extra on the side."

"Good, I think it will be great for all involved. Have you and Lindy discussed salaries?"

"No, she said she would leave that up to you."

"Since you will be running the tennis program solo, how about fifty?"

"That is more than fair and much better than I am bringing in now," Elin said.

"Very good, so what equipment will you need?"

Elin left Marley with a list and the name of a local supplier. She only needed to give a week's notice at the country club, so she would be available to start sooner than Marley had expected. "I'm sure Luna could use an extra set of hands to get some of the equipment set up and I'm certain there will be plenty to keep you busy until we open."

"This is so exciting," Elin said as they walked back inside and up the stairs to the flats.

"I will be living on-site to provide some added security as well as to paint the ruse that the flats are used as rentals," she explained as they walked downstairs to find Luna speaking with the next group of applicants.

Luna looked up when she saw them come down the stairs and Marley gave her a nod. She introduced the two women she was talking with. "This is Marley, our club manager and Elin, our tennis director. Ladies this is Pepper and Haley. Pepper is a fitness trainer, and Haley is an all-around office guru."

"Nice to meet you all. I will give you a call later in the week to arrange schedules," Elin said to Marley and left.

"Why don't you show the ladies around the club and we will meet back here," Marley suggested as she walked back to her office.

"Sure thing, Boss." Luna took the ladies on a tour.

Marley flipped on the light and was surprised to find her office fully furnished. There was a note on the cherry wood desk from Lindy. *'I hope you find this suitable. If not, we can exchange anything you don't approve of, including the chair. I tried it out and it seemed very comfy to me.'*

The furnishings were finer than anything Marley had ever had, she sat down at her desk to try out the chair and it indeed was very comfortable. She smiled as she tore the note from the tablet and folded it and placed it in her center drawer.

She walked out to retrieve her briefcase and notepad to begin making a list of clothing and shoe sizes. She settled in to her office while she waited for Luna to return with the two women. When she heard them approach, she returned to the front room.

"What do you think, Ladies?" she asked.

"This is going to be a wonderful place," Pepper said.

"Yes it is, Pepper. Do you want to be a part of it?"

"I most certainly do."

Marley looked at Haley who was also nodding her head. "Luna, can I see you in my office for a minute? Will you excuse us, Ladies?"

Luna followed Marley into the office. "What do you recommend for salaries?"

"I would say forty for Pepper and thirty for Haley."

"You have explained everything to them, especially the discretion they will need to display."

"They are completely aware," Luna assured her.

"Very well, send Pepper back first then."

"Yes, Ma'am," Luna left the room.

Marley made the offers and both women heartily accepted their new positions. Luna added their names to the list and got their sizes for the uniforms Lindy would be ordering. Marley was sure Luna had talked to them about complete discretion, but she wanted to hear it for herself. "I want to make sure that you two understand about the activities upstairs. Luna and I are single, so we don't have to worry about a jealous partner. You won't be able to participate directly Haley, since you will be managing the reception area and acting as our first line of security, but Pepper will." She paused to allow her words to sink in. "Do either of you have a problem with this? I would understand if you needed time to discuss this before you give us a final answer."

Haley looked at Pepper and then smiled at Marley. "Business is business, and this is too good of an offer for us to pass on. I trust that Pepper only has me in her heart."

"Very well then. Welcome aboard, Ladies."

When the two women left, Marley looked at Luna. "Things are shaping up quickly, aren't they?"

"Yeah, we just need the massage therapists and we will be good to go."

"I have three scheduled for this afternoon and the first should be here soon."

"You think we could be fully staffed by the end of today?" Luna asked.

"That's the plan."

"Sweet." Luna smiled broadly.

"If we have everyone on board in two weeks that will give us a full week to make sure everything is in place for the grand opening."

"Pepper is between positions right now so I have asked her to come in this week and help me with the equipment set up. I hope that's okay."

"That's perfect," Marley assured her.

By the end of the afternoon they were indeed fully staffed. Marley turned to Luna. "This was a productive day. Would you care to join me for some dinner?"

"That would be awesome."

"I think I'm in the mood for some Sushi. How about you?"

"Sushi sounds great. I know just the perfect place, but I insist on buying."

"I have no problem with that. Let's lock up here and I'll follow you."

CHAPTER FIVE

The next morning Luna met Marley at the local fitness equipment company and when they left there was an agreement to begin delivering the equipment on Wednesday after the flooring was finished. There were a few pieces of equipment that would need to be ordered, but they were promised for delivery by Friday.

Luna was unable to sit still when they returned to the club and Marley gave her a list of items to order after she left for work at the clinic. Pepper pulled up just as Marley was leaving to help Luna with the ordering of supplies.

"I will see you both later tonight," Marley said as she walked from the club. "Have a great day."

"You too," Luna said. "We will be thinking about you slaving away at the clinic."

"I will be dreaming about this place." Marley climbed in behind the wheel.

Tom's crew was busy installing the flooring and Luna couldn't help herself from walking back to the fitness room to check on the progress. She was very pleased at the appearance and the pace the men were working.

"What do you think?" Tom asked.

"This looks great. Will it be settled enough to put heavy equipment on it by Wednesday?"

"You could put it on tomorrow with no problems. This is the best flooring money can buy. Mrs. Freemont has only gone with the best on this project."

"Yes, she has," Luna agreed with a smile and returned to the office to continue ordering supplies.

Later in the afternoon, equipment and supplies began rolling in. The equipment for the laundry was delivered and set up just as Pepper returned bringing in the linens they had ordered. The electrician had finished hard wiring the alarms and camera system and internet was run throughout the building. Flat screen televisions were delivered and installed and by the time Marley returned after her last appointment, the empty rooms were starting to take shape.

The flooring crew stayed late to finish the floors. Luna was standing in the doorway of her exercise haven watching the final piece being laid when Marley walked in. Luna was lost in thought and did not hear her approach.

"This is looking great." She stopped beside Luna.

Luna jumped in surprise. "Sorry, I didn't hear you come in. Yeah, it is looking great."

Marley leaned against the doorframe. "I called my landlord today and he was pleased with the idea of you subletting the apartment."

"That's great news," Luna eyes glowed with excitement. "I can't wait to have my own place."

Marley smiled at her excitement. "I will start moving tonight if you help me load and transport some stuff."

"You have a deal."

"Toss in supper and I will volunteer to help," Pepper said as she stopped beside them. "Let me give Hayley a call and let her know I'll be late."

"Do you want to invite her to join us?" Luna asked.

"Naw, she detests moving, but thanks."

"Italian then, Ladies?" Marley asked.

"Sounds wonderful to me," Luna said. "I could use some carbohydrates."

"The crew here is just about done. Why don't you grab some food and Pepper and I will meet you at the apartment?"

"Any special requests," she asked.

"Food and lots of it," Pepper said. "We haven't eaten all day."

"What? You didn't even take a lunch break?"

"Nope, we were too busy, Boss. Want me to show you around really quick?"

Marley followed Luna through the laundry room and back to her office. She opened a small closet door and inside was five sets of new uniforms. "Those came out really nice."

"Yeah they did. They were delivered already pressed this afternoon," Luna answered.

Marley was still staring at the uniforms, "This is really happening, isn't it, Luna?"

"Yes, it is, Boss. Do I need to pinch you?"

Marley turned to look at Luna who was grinning broadly. "No, but it all does seem like a dream sometimes."

"I agree, but even if it's a dream, it's a really good one." Marley left Luna and Pepper to lock up after the workers finished, while she went to pick up some dinner for them. She called her favorite Italian restaurant and placed an order as she drove and hoped she wouldn't have to wait too long to pick it up. She had decided to leave all of her furniture for Luna, so she would just need to take clothing and her personal belongings to the club. They could make a large dent in the move tonight she thought as she waited for a traffic light to turn green.

†

"Let's take these boxes over to Marley's," Luna suggested as they made a final pass through the club before leaving. "I doubt she has given any consideration to moving boxes."

"Probably not as busy as she's been," Pepper agreed. "Toss them in my backseat and you can leave your bike and ride with me if you want."

She and Pepper drove to Marley's apartment and were unloading the boxes when she arrived. "That was great timing," Marley said as she climbed out of her car. "Come help me with this Luna."

Luna walked over to her car and whistled loudly when she saw the bags of food loaded in the back seat. "You plan on feeding an army?"

"You claimed you were hungry."

"Yeah, but if we eat all of this there won't be any packing and moving done tonight."

"No way, I'm getting my money's worth out of you two tonight," Marley fired back. "Besides, I have decided to leave the furniture for you to use which should make the move much easier."

"We might have you all moved tonight then."

Marley laughed loudly. "You obviously haven't seen my closets then."

"Oh please, don't tell me you are one of those women who have a pair of shoes to match every outfit!"

Pepper punched her in the arm. "What's wrong with that?"

"Dear God, not you too," Luna said with exaggerated desperation.

Pepper carried the boxes inside and Marley pointed her to the bedroom. "Just drop them in there and come eat." She and Luna began placing food containers on the small table.

Luna moaned with the opening of each container. "I can feel a very long work out coming on to burn up these calories."

"I told you I planned to work you hard tonight," Marley said, just as her phone began to ring. She looked at the number. "Lindy."

"This is Marley."

"Hello Marley, this is Lindy. I just wanted to say I stopped by the club tonight and things are looking great."

"Thanks. Luna and Pepper worked all day getting the deliveries taken care of and orders placed. I have them here now and after we eat some dinner, they are going to help me move some personal stuff to the club."

"That's great to hear. I would feel more comfortable having someone on site at night until we get up and running."

"I should be all moved by tomorrow night," Marley said.

"Do you need any help?"

"No, but we would love it if you stopped by and had dinner with us, if you haven't eaten yet."

Marley could see the mischief light up in Luna's eyes when she invited Lindy to dinner.

"I'd love to, but Jay Dub is flying in tonight. I will drop by the club tomorrow night, so hopefully I will see you then."

"That sounds wonderful. See you then."

"Is she coming by?" Luna asked.

"No. Her husband is returning home. She said she would stop by the club tomorrow night and was very pleased with the progress you two made today."

†

After they put a dent in the food, Luna and Pepper began carrying out her hang up clothing from the closet while Marley started boxing up clothing items from her dressers. "Should we go ahead and take this shoe rack and all these shoes?" Luna asked.

"Sure," Marley said. "You can toss all the shoes in a garbage bag and place the rack in my backseat."

"We will be ready to take the first load in just a few minutes then," Luna yelled as she went to the kitchen for a garbage bag.

Marley had emptied the contents of her dressers into three of the boxes. Her bedroom was already looking bare and lonely she thought as she sealed up the last of the boxes and handed it to Luna to carry out to the car. She was excited about her new home, but would miss the small little apartment that she had called home for a several years. There were a lot of good memories between these walls. She walked into the kitchen where Pepper and Luna waited for her.

"Let's put these leftovers in the fridge and we can finish them off tomorrow night," Marley said as she looked at her watch. "Let's drop this load and then call it a night."

"No problem, Boss," Luna said. "Do you want me to bring some newspaper over tomorrow for packing your dishes?"

"I'm going to leave the dishes and kitchenware for you, so I shouldn't need a lot," Marley said.

"You got a sweet deal going on here," Pepper said as she bumped into Luna. "I wish Haley and I could land a deal like this."

"I must be doing something right," Luna winked at Marley.

Pepper placed the last of the containers in the fridge and they drove back to the club. They all carried an armful up the stairs to Marley's corner unit. She had carried a box from her dresser filled with undergarments and sat them on the bed.

"Why don't you unload your box while Pepper and I carry the rest up?"

"That would be great." Marley began unpacking the box and placing her clothes in the chest of drawers in the bedroom as Luna and Pepper made four more trips each to bring in the rest of her clothes and shoes.

"I put your shoe rack in the closet and Pepper is finishing placing your shoes back in order. Do you want us to help put the rest away?"

"No, thanks, you have both done so much already tonight. I'm going to empty these last two boxes and then head for home myself."

"We should get the rest of your stuff moved tomorrow night then," Luna said.

"Will you need help moving your stuff in, Luna?" Pepper asked.

"Lord no, all I have is some clothes and a few other items. Thankfully Marley is selling me her furniture. One trip in a friend's truck, and I'll be moved."

"I need to clean the place up for you first."

"That's the least I can do in appreciation for all that you have done for me. Besides, the place is pretty much spotless already."

"Thanks, you two," Marley hugged each of her friends and said goodnight to them.

"I'll lock the door behind us," Luna said as they disappeared down the stairs.

"Thanks," Marley called after them.

Marley sat on the edge of the king-sized bed and looked around her new bedroom. The rooms were well furnished with designer lines, but the walls were left bare. Marley visually planned where she would hang her artwork and then went to work unpacking the rest of her clothing. She smirked when she placed a well-worn night shirt in the drawer. "Time to do some shopping," she said aloud and giggled. When she finished, she walked down the stairs to her office. She flipped on the light and her eyes came to rest on the desk where a small gift sat wrapped on top of a card. She walked over and picked up the card. She opened it and found a hand-written note from Lindy.

Thanks for everything you and the ladies have done so far in making my dreams come true.
Lindy

Marley was eager to see what the small box held, but carefully removed the expensive wrapping paper and slipped the lid from the box to reveal a beautiful black Movado watch. Marley had been drooling over the exact watch for years, but her limited income had never allowed her to afford such a luxury. She took the watch from the felt lined box and turned it over in her hands marveling at the beauty of the piece before slipping it over her wrist. It fit perfectly, and tears welled in her eyes. She felt a pang of guilt for accepting such an expensive gift, but she knew that Lindy would be offended if she balked at accepting her offering. She would find a way to pay her back for the generosity of the gift.

She turned off the lights as she moved back through the club and locked the door behind her as she started for home to spend her last night in her tiny apartment. For a brief moment, she felt a hint of remorse about leaving the place she had called home for several years, but the spaciousness of her new flat brought on a whole new feeling of excitement. It was by far the largest space she had lived in since leaving home.

Once she locked the door of her apartment behind her, she walked to her bedroom, stripping out of her clothes as she made her way to the shower. Only a few more miserable days left at work she promised herself as she showered and dressed for bed. She felt herself smiling at the memory of sleeping next to Luna, and she hoped Luna would enjoy the apartment as much as she had over the years she had lived there. It was a perfect location. Not far from the club, but when Lindy offered up the corner flat, Marley knew it was too good of an opportunity to pass. "I must be doing something right too," she said, mimicking Luna's comment from earlier.

CHAPTER SIX

Her boss surprised her when she got to work the following morning. "Today is your last day Marley," he said.

"What do you mean? I still have the rest of my notice to work out."

"Nope, I received a call from Lindy Freemont, and she bought out the rest of your notice. I don't know what you fed that woman, but she thinks very highly of you. We're going to miss you being here."

Marley just smiled at his comment and went to her work station and began packing up her goods. She was eager to finish her last two appointments and be on her way. Her first appointment arrived and the hour passed quickly. Marley was about to break for lunch when the receptionist called to inform her that her last appointment had called and cancelled. She quickly packed the remainder of her belongings and dropped her keys off to her boss before heading out the door.

"Good luck," her boss said as she walked quickly away. Marley tossed her hand up in a wave and kept moving.

Feeling better than she had in many years, Marley drove to the club. Luna and Pepper were busily discussing the work out area, and in between deliveries they had been stocking linens and other supplies.

"Fancy seeing you here this early," Luna said when she saw Marley walk in carrying a box. "Do you need some help?"

"Yeah, I got a couple other boxes in the back seat."

"Are you on lunch break?" Pepper asked.

Marley smiled. "No ma'am, Lindy bought out my notice from the clinic."

"Damn, that woman really likes you," Luna teased.

"As a matter of fact, I do," said Lindy who had surprised all of them by walking in so quietly. "I have every intention of working her just as hard though. When you finish bringing in your boxes, join me in your office, please."

"Go ahead, we will get the boxes and place them in your flat," Luna said.

"Thanks, Ladies," Marley said and followed Lindy to her office in the rear of the club. Once inside the office she turned to face Lindy. "Thanks for buying out my contract. My heart really wasn't into being there this week."

"I can understand that, besides we have a lot of work to do."

"Where do we start?"

"I took the liberty of having some software pre-loaded onto the desktop computer. I want to spend the afternoon teaching you how to use it."

"Sounds good to me," Marley sat in the chair in front of the computer. The watch was on her wrist and she turned to show it to Lindy. "Thanks for this beautiful gift."

"It was my pleasure. I hope you like it."

"I've been drooling over this watch for years. It's perfect."

"Alright then. Let's start by setting up the payroll file and getting these ladies on payroll," Lindy passed a stack of forms over to Marley.

Within an hour, Lindy had walked Marley through the process of adding staff to payroll for processing and they loaded time sheets for each of the staff onto a laptop that would be placed at the front desk.

"At the close of every week you link up to the payroll company and transmit the files for payment. Within twelve hours, the funds will be transferred directly into their checking accounts and the payroll stubs will automatically print on your printer."

"That's amazing."

"All you have to do after you hit send is to print and place their pay stubs in an envelope and put them in their boxes."

"That seems simple enough. What's next?"

"I have set up a preliminary budget for the club. Let's pull that up next and print a copy for you."

Lindy walked Marley through each step of entering the invoices they had received for the club start-up expenses. "You are actually under budget for start-up expenses so far," Lindy said when they printed out a statement. "Let's take a break and then we can finish up later."

Marley welcomed a break and stood to stretch.

Lindy smiled at her. "Not used to sitting still for that long?"

"No, not really, I spend most of the day on my feet."

"Let's go check on the ladies and see if they are ready for some lunch."

Marley followed Lindy into the reception area. They found Luna and Pepper drafting a work out record. They looked up and smiled at Lindy and Marley. "Hey Marley, can you work on something for us?"

"Sure, what do you need?"

"We have a rough draft of a work out record, but we need someone to make it look professional before we send it out to the printers. Would you help?" Luna asked.

"That seems easy enough. I will tackle it after lunch. I'm starving."

"I think we all could use a break. How about some sushi, my treat?" Lindy asked

"Oh yeah," Luna said. "I have to warn you, I'm starving too."

Lindy looked at Marley. "I think you will need to drive. I believe you are the only one who can comfortably seat four."

"That's no problem," Marley dug out her keys and they walked out to the parking lot. "What are the guys working on today?" she asked Luna.

"One crew is putting the finishing touches on the sauna and another is working on the Roman bath." The design on the bath is totally awesome I might add."

"Maybe we should try out the sauna later, just to make sure everything works, of course," Lindy suggested.

"I think we could all use some relaxation later," Marley agreed.

"You won't get any argument from me," Pepper said.

"Oh, I'm all in," Luna added.

They feasted on sushi for lunch and when they were done, Lindy told them she had some errands to run, but that she would be back later so they could try out the sauna.

Luna and Marley watched her leave the club and then entered behind Pepper.

"If you will give me that work out record, I will take a stab at it," Marley said as they entered the reception area.

Pepper walked into the room, "You need to come and take a look at this."

The group followed her into the Roman Bath area and was amazed at the intricate tile that Tom's crew had finished installing. "This is gorgeous," Marley said as she bent down for a closer inspection.

"It needs a few days to cure, but we should have it filled and the water heated by this time Friday," Tom said as he re-entered the room.

"You guys are amazing," Luna said.

"The electrician will be here in a few minutes to finish out the security system and then you ladies should be good to go," he said with a warm smile.

"You really have done an amazing job," Marley said.

"I hope Lindy will pass on a good recommendation to her circle if they need contractor services."

"I am quite certain you would come highly recommended after the job you have done here," Marley assured him.

He walked around the bath with her and then led her to the completed sauna. "This was actually a fun project to work on and quite challenging to get it done so quickly."

Their tour was interrupted by the arrival of the electrician and Marley returned to her office to begin drafting the form for Luna and Pepper. The form was actually pretty simple to make and after an hour of fine tuning the layout she was ready to make the presentation to them.

Both Luna and Pepper were pleased with the design and Marley handed Pepper a credit card with instructions to take the design to the nearest print shop and have them make the cards they needed for start-up.

She took the printout of the start-up budget and reviewed it with Luna. "We have come in significantly under what Lindy had allowed for start-up. Is there anything we are missing?"

Luna and Marley walked room by room to make a mental assessment of equipment and supplies. "Other than a few more decorations, I think we are set," Luna said.

"You must have been reading my mind," Lindy walked in carrying an armful of pictures to hang on the walls. "Be a dear, Luna, and get the rest out of the car for me, please."

"Yes, Ma'am," Luna trotted to the door.

"We were just doing a walk through to see if there was anything we were missing," Marley told Lindy.

"I think these should just about do it, but if we need more, just go get what you need," she placed the pictures on the reception desk.

Luna came back in carrying a large number of framed prints and added them to the pile on the reception desk.

"Luna and I will hang them if you will decide where they should go." Luna went to the back to retrieve some tools.

Lindy picked up print after print and placed them in each of the rooms. "Wait until we have them all laid out before you start hanging them."

She, Luna and Pepper who had returned from her errand followed Lindy through the club to assist with placements and when they were done, Luna and Marley began to hang the pictures. Lindy was talking with Tom about the security system and when he got into the details of operating the system, she called them over to listen.

When he had concluded the orientation, Tom took his leave and Lindy followed him to the door and locked it behind him. They all watched her and when she turned back found them smiling at her. "Pepper, if you will help me, we can speed up the picture hanging and get on to the fun stuff. I really want to try out that sauna."

Within thirty minutes, the pictures were hung and they all converged on the sauna. It was larger than Marley had originally thought and could easily accommodate a dozen women. Eager to begin, Lindy said, "Crank her up Marley and let's go get out of these clothes."

Marley turned the dial to begin heating the sauna and they all walked to the dressing room to strip out of their clothes and wrap their bodies in thick towels. Luna and Marley took advantage of the upper benches while Pepper and Lindy stretched out on the lower level.

"This feels heavenly," Lindy said as the perspiration began running down her body.
"What a great way to end a good day."

"Amen to that," Marley said as she closed her eyes and relaxed.

"What are the plans for the rest of the week?" Lindy asked.

"The last of the equipment will be delivered on Friday and will take a good two days to set up," Luna said.

"The rest of the staff is due to begin work on Monday, so we will need to begin orientation to the club," Marley said.

"Can Luna and Pepper handle that?" Lindy asked.

"Yes, I'm sure they can," Marley said.

"Good, you and I need to finish up some training on the financials, and then spend a few days visiting with caterers in preparation for the grand opening event."

"Sounds like a plan to me."

"Some of the clientele are itching to get started. Do you think by mid-week next week we could start setting up some evaluation appointments and maybe some massages?"

Marley looked at Luna who grinned and nodded her head. "I don't see a problem with that at all."

"Good, I think it would be nice if some of the ladies could benefit from the services prior to the grand opening, that way they are familiar with the club and staff."

Leave it to Luna to ask the obvious question Marley thought. "Does that go for upstairs activities as well?"

Lindy chuckled. "Truth be known, I think that is the activity they are looking forward to the most."

Luna grinned. It was possible that it was the service she would most enjoy as well.

Lindy stretched in the heat of the sauna. "I really miss my weekly massages, Marley. Do you think you would have time for one tonight?"

"No problem at all," Marley said as the timer kicked off ending the session. "Why don't you shower and I will get the massage table set up? When I've run through a quick shower, I'll be ready too."

"You have a deal, young lady," Lindy headed for the locker room.

†

"We will see you back here at nine, Marley." Luna said. "Pepper is helping me move in to the apartment tonight. I hope you enjoy your first night here."

"I'm looking forward to it," Marley said as they parted ways. "See you in the morning."

Marley walked into the main massage room and turned on some low lighting and started the oil warmer. She turned on soft relaxing panpipe music and poured fresh aromatic oil in a burner. Satisfied that the room was prepared, she climbed the stairs to her flat for fresh clothing. She entered the locker room just as Luna and Pepper were leaving. "Good-night! We'll lock the door behind us."

"Thanks," Marley said and reached in to start the water in a shower.

Lindy was wrapped in a fresh clean towel. "I will wait for you in the massage room," she said as Marley dropped the towel in a hamper.

"I will be there in just a few minutes."

"Take your time," Lindy said and left the locker room.

Marley stripped down and stepped into the warm shower. The water washed away the remnants of the sauna and the last bit of tension from the long day and she found that she actually felt eager to give Lindy a massage. After so many years, it felt odd to not have her hands on bodies, kneading muscles all day long. She felt a smile grow on her face as she wondered if Lindy had other services on her mind as well. She shut down the shower and dried before slipping into a clean outfit.

She walked to the massage area and gently knocked on the closed door. "Lindy, are you ready for me to come in?"

"Ready and waiting," Lindy's voice already sounding relaxed.

Marley walked in and found Lindy lying on her stomach covered with a fresh sheet. "Are there any particular sensitive spots I need to work on?"

Lindy chuckled softly. "There are plenty, but those will wait for later if you're up to it," unknowingly answering the question Marley had asked herself.

"Certainly." Marley returned Lindy's smile.

Marley coated Lindy's back with warm oils and deeply massaged the tense muscles. "Are you on your own tonight?"

"Yes, Jay Dub and some of his cronies are having a poker night, so I probably won't see him until he comes stumbling in around midnight."

Marley noticed a slight sadness to Lindy's tone when she talked about her husband and decided to steer clear of the subject. "I think you made Luna's day by suggesting some private assessments for some of the ladies next week."

"She is a fireball," Lindy said with a contented purr to her voice. "Have you ever been with her?"

"With Luna? No, we are just good friends."

"Girl you should give her a shot. I know she is very interested in you."

That comment surprised Marley. "What makes you think that?"

"She idolizes you. When you are in the room, she watches everything you do, with more than just a casual interest."

"Roll over for me," Marley let Lindy's words sink in. With a deep sigh that surprised even her, she said, "Luna can have any woman she sets her eyes on and I don't think she is ready to settle down."

"Is that really such a bad thing? Settling down I mean. Luna seems to really enjoy her life and lifestyle so why should she be in a hurry to settle down?"

"Oh no, I think it's perfect for Luna, and yes she really enjoys life, but I think that is what has kept us on a friend's only status."

"You are more of a one-person woman?"

"Yes, and sometimes then I have difficulty with one," Marley chuckled.

"Well, maybe your time here at the club will help you relax and enjoy life a little more." Marley's hands smoothed the warm oil over her stomach causing her to moan softly.

"You certainly know how to bring pleasure to a woman's body."

Marley smiled at the comment and slipped out of her clothes under the watchful eye of Lindy. She removed the sheet and began to climb onto the end of the massage table raising an eyebrow from Lindy. She grasped the bottle of warm oil and squeezed it allowing the oil to slide down the front of her body and then dribbled a fresh line down the front of Lindy's body causing her to shiver with delight. Marley positioned herself between Lindy's legs and leaned forward to press her body onto her. The fresh oil mixed between their bodies and a slow undulating movement spread the heated oil across their skin as Marley lowered her lips onto Lindy's.

A groan escaped Lindy as their tongues met and their bodies glided together. Her hands found Marley's hips pulling her closer as they entwined in a lover's embrace, skin gliding across skin. Marley teased Lindy with her body and mouth until she was sure Lindy was desperate for release, then she moved off the table and pulled Lindy to the edge. Her mouth parted silky lips to enter Lindy with her tongue, as her hands continued to stroke and tease Lindy's nipples. Her hips writhed in pleasure as Marley's tongue explored her completely, and when Marley slipped a finger inside her wetness, Lindy exploded, filling Marley's hand with her sweet nectar. She shuddered with release for several moments as Marley gently stroked her body.

Lindy slowly propped up on her elbows and looked down at a smiling Marley. "Luna has nothing on you," she purred, completely content.

"We have different techniques, so it depends on what you need."

Lindy broke out in a fit of laughter. "Luna is definitely not ten humps and a slump."

"No, I bet she's not," Marley stood and offered a hand to Lindy. "Ready for a shower?"

"I think I can make it that far."

"You need help showering?"

"That's an offer I can't refuse," Lindy allowed Marley to lead her into a shower.

Marley easily brought Lindy to orgasm against the wall of the shower with a deep shudder. After that, Lindy indeed needed assistance to bathe herself and dress before leaving the club.

"I will sleep like a baby tonight." A contented smile playing on Lindy's lips.

"I don't think I will have any problem either."

"You are staying here tonight, correct?"

"Yes, my first night here."

"Do you have plans for dinner?"

"I thought I would make a run out to get something. I haven't gone to the grocery store yet."

"What would you like?"

"I'm starved, but not real picky."

"I would love to take you out to celebrate, but to be honest I probably couldn't stay awake for it, but would you mind if I had something delivered for you?"

"You don't have to do that Lindy."

"I know, but it would please me greatly."

"Very well then." Marley slipped shorts and a t-shirt on.

Lindy was fully dressed. "Just answer the door when it arrives. I will order for you on my way home." She left the locker room. "Enjoy dinner, and I will see you tomorrow."

"Thanks again." Marley walked her to the door. She returned to the massage room to straighten it up and found three hundred-dollar bills sitting on the counter by her watch. She smiled and slipped the bills into her pocket and wiped down the table and checked the locker room while she waited on the food.

Thirty minutes later the intercom on the front door was activated and she walked to the door. A young waiter stood at the door with an armload of food. "Are you Marley?"

"Yes, I am."

"Your meal then, Ma'am," he offered her the bags of food.

"I didn't know you delivered," she said when she noticed that the food was coming from Victor's, a very elite steak house. The same one, Lindy took her to that first night.

"We don't ma'am, except to a very few select clientele." He smiled at a speechless Marley.

Marley settled the bags in one hand and went to take a tip out of her pocket. "Nothing needed ma'am, everything has been covered."

"Thanks." She closed the door behind her. Marley carried the bags into the juice bar and found they contained a huge T-bone steak, salad, baked potato and a half gallon bottle of sweet tea. The aroma of the steak made her groan and she went to work on consuming the food, eating her fill before climbing up the stairs to store her leftovers and relax before bedtime.

CHAPTER SEVEN

Marley woke the next morning from a deep relaxing slumber to a feeling of disorientation, until she remembered that she wasn't dreaming, that she was truly living in a luxurious flat, with a fantastic new job and no more financial worries. She looked above the bed through the skylight to see the first rays of sunlight reaching her view, filling the air with brilliant hues of orange and yellow as the sun's rays reflected off the changing leaves of the trees surrounding the building. She stretched on the comfortable bed, the mattress contouring around her form. She didn't remember a better night's sleep. Normally, her bed linens would be disheveled from the night spent tossing and turning, but scanning the bed, there was little evidence she had moved at all during the night.

She tossed the down comforter off her and felt a chill in the air. She grinned as she spoke a command to the automated system. "Increase the temperature by four degrees." A whisper quiet swoosh indicated the system had kicked on. *I will be spoiled by all this technology.* "Television on to the Weather Channel." Just in time for the local forecast, she heard the report of clear skies for the next three days before a cool front moved into the region. She walked to the window to gaze out, and the newly surfaced green tennis court glowed in the morning light. Perhaps the only thing Lindy hadn't thought about was tennis once the weather turned cool. She made a mental note to ask Lindy if she had made other arrangements for the short winter months.

Marley rubbed the sleep from her eyes and walked to her bathroom. "Set water temp in the shower to one hundred twelve." She chuckled as the steam began to form in the enclosure and stripped out of her nightshirt. The flow of steamy water from three heads caressed her body, Marley felt invigorated from the great night's sleep and the wonderful shower. She stepped out of the flow and opened the door as the water turned off. The bath sheets Lindy had stocked the flat with were soft against her skin as she wrapped it around her body and walked over to her closet. When she opened the door, she was surprised to see six pairs of turquoise athletic slacks and peach oxford shirts with the club logo. She could imagine Lindy describing them as "more professional attire for the club manager." If Lindy wanted her to look more professional, then that's exactly what she will get. Further examination of the closet revealed several black and brown leather belts and two pairs of dressy loafers to match the belts. Marley hummed to herself as she completed her morning hygiene and slipped into perfectly fitting clothes. She looked at her image in the full-length mirror. "Yeah, I can get used to this look."

She walked back into the kitchen and poured a glass of juice and dropped a bagel into the toaster. She instructed the television to turn to a local news channel. The name Freemont caught her attention on the local news, and she turned to see the image of Judge Freemont flash across the screen as they reported on the beginning of a new federal case he would be presiding over. He was a handsome man, with finely coiffed salt and pepper hair, and brilliant blue eyes. He had the type of charisma and smile that could win the hearts of others easily. A gorgeous young prosecutor stood close beside him, and Marley wondered if the young lawyer was one of his mistresses. She wasn't sure if Lindy would be pleased, or disappointed, that he would be at home for the next few weeks, possibly months, as the trial proceeded.

†

Marley sat at her desk reviewing the software Lindy was teaching her to use. She had drained her coffee and was about to leave the office for a refill when Lindy entered. She smiled when she saw her dressed in her new clothing.

"Good morning. You look very nice."

"Thanks, Boss. I think I'll let you make all my clothing purchases in the future. These fit and feel great." Marley stood and turned around to model her new look.

"I have a feeling most anything would look good on you."

Marley felt the heat rising up her neck. "I was about to get a refill," holding up her coffee mug. "Would you care for some?"

"I'd love some. I put a case of new mugs on the counter. I thought some with the club's logo would be nice."

"You've thought of everything. I do have one question though." She watched Lindy cock her head as she waited. "I know we have a relatively mild winter usually, but what plans do you have for tennis lessons when it turns too cold to be outside?"

Lindy smiled. "Elin has already made arrangements with an indoor practice court at one of the local clubs. If we are as successful as I hope, we can add an indoor court of our own with heating and cooling sources."

"I knew you would have arrangements. I'll be right back."

Marley walked to the coffee bar and opened the case of new mugs and rinsed out two before pouring their drinks. She glanced at the clock. Luna and Pepper would be arriving soon to continue to set up equipment. Maybe they could begin setting up some appointments for assessments if Lindy could give them contact information. She picked up the mugs and returned to the office. Lindy had pulled up a chair next to the desk. She placed the mugs down on coasters. "Here we go."

"Mmm, there's nothing like the smell of rich coffee."

Lindy's voice was a soft purr early in the morning. Marley felt her blood rushing as her nose filled with the soft perfume Lindy wore. She sat in the chair next to her. "I was thinking. Luna and Pepper have almost all the equipment set up until the final order arrives tomorrow. What do you think about them making some calls to set up assessments? Orientation should only take a day next week."

"I do love the way you think. I've installed a file of client contacts. If you pull it up, you can print two copies for them to start making the calls."

Marley pulled up the files and made the copies as they enjoyed their coffee. Lindy walked her through a few more spreadsheets and financial reports until they heard the distinct rumble of Luna's bike. A few minutes later, Luna strolled in wearing turquoise sweats and a t-shirt. Looking delicious as usual. Marley couldn't help but smile at the way Lindy appreciated the view, as Luna leaned against the doorframe.

"Morning. Ladies," she grinned. "What do you have planned for us today, Boss?"

"Lindy and I thought between your setting up the last of the equipment, you and Pepper could start making contacts to set up assessments next week, starting Tuesday after we complete staff orientation."

"Do we have to wait that long? The last of the equipment will arrive Friday, but Pepper and I can set it up Saturday."

Marley looked to Lindy, who shrugged. "Fine by me. I know a few of them are aching to get started. Are you up to a few massages, Marley?"

"Sure, I can't let my hands get lazy," she chuckled.

"Have at it then," Lindy handed Luna the printed copies. "I have one request."

Luna took the pages, "What's that, Boss?"

"Start with Danna Nichols. She's a recent widow, and could probably use a good massage, and maybe some special attention from you Luna."

Luna grinned. "She'll be my first call. Can you be ready to do a massage by three, Marley?"

"I should be ready by then unless Lindy has other plans."

"We should be done with our catering meeting no later than one. We're meeting for lunch, so that should work well."

Luna turned at the sound of the front door opening. "Pepper is here so we'll finish with the equipment and get started with the calls."

When Luna left, Marley turned back to Lindy. "Are there any specifics we should know about our clients? Like Mrs. Nichols, who is recently widowed, so we don't make any embarrassing blunders."

Lindy tilted her head as she thought. Marley thought she was adorable when she was pondering ideas. "This weekend, I'll spend some time developing client profiles that we can share with the group during orientation Monday."

"That sounds perfect. What else do you need to teach me?"

"There is some additional human resource stuff I want to go over with you in preparation for Monday. I've got us set up with a health insurance carrier and an investment firm for a 401K plan. I've got packets of information we need to get filled out, and I thought we could start with yours. The club is covering each of you with life insurance equal to your annual salary, but there are still beneficiary forms and personal information to complete."

Lindy reached for her satchel and pulled out a file folder. "There's a lot of paper. Why don't we go into the lounge to spread them out on a table? Grab a pen and follow me."

They spent the next thirty minutes filling out benefit forms. When it was time to designate a beneficiary and emergency contact information, Marley entered her brother's information. Lindy watched her carefully and when she finished writing, she smiled at Marley. "You know, this makes me realize I don't know much about you. You know so much about me, but I know very little about you."

Marley returned her smile. "There's not much to share. Charles is my younger brother and only sibling. He lives in Montgomery, Alabama, and has two wonderful sons and a beautiful wife."

"Do you get to see them often?"

"Not as often as I'd like. They are growing up so fast. I do try to visit over Thanksgiving and Christmas when I can."

"Is that where you're from?"

"Columbus, Georgia, originally. I came to Atlanta for college and massage school and never left."

"Do your parents still live there?"

"No, it's just my brother and me. Alzheimer's took dad after mom died from cancer."

Lindy covered her hand with her smaller one. "I'm sorry. I hope I didn't dredge up sad memories for you."

Marley shook her head. "It's been some time ago, but I miss them both dearly."

"I understand. I lost both of my parents, and I am an only child."

"Are you a native of Atlanta?"

"Born and raised. I wandered up to Athens for college where I met my husband. He was working for a local law firm and after we married, he took a position back here in Atlanta."

"Any kids?"

"Not for me, but Jay Dub has a daughter from his previous marriage Susan. She's a nurse practitioner and is doing some missionary work in Haiti right now."

"Wow, he must be proud of her."

"We are. I'm happy she's following her heart to care for others, instead of chasing the almighty dollar."

"Do you get to see her often?"

"A couple of times a year. She will be home for Christmas. I'd love for you to meet her. I think you two would hit it off."

"Oh really? How so?"

"For starters, both single lesbians," Lindy answered with a chuckle. "You both have huge giving hearts."

Marley chuckled. "Does she have any idea about TWC?"

"She thinks it's a great idea. We talked about it a few months ago. She's no more pleased with her father's behavior than I am."

"I can imagine. I would like to meet her."

"I think she's a few years older, actually she's only five years younger than me, but I think you would hit it off."

"Is that strange for her that her stepmom is so close to her age?"

"We've never discussed it. We get along pretty well. For the short amount of time we get to spend together."

Marley chuckled and shook her head. "How do you think she'd react with me giving pleasure to her stepmother?"

"Susan's a pretty open-minded free spirit. I guess only time will tell though."

Luna walked in and the personal conversation ended, much to Marley's relief.

"You have a massage scheduled for three with Mrs. Nichols," Luna told Marley. "She'll be here at two for a fitness assessment and to set some fitness goals with me."

Lindy smiled at Luna's excitement. "Are your contacts going well?"

"Very well, we're going to busy next week."

"Do you mind if I go out and purchase some appointment books?" Luna asked. "My post-it-note filing system isn't working."

Lindy broke out laughing. "I knew there was something I was forgetting. Yes, go ahead and I'll order everyone nice ones with the club logo. Once Haley comes on board, we'll add appointment calendars to the computer system, but it will still be nice for each of you to have access to one."

"Do you want me to take care of that?"

"That would be great, Luna. Let me download the logo onto a jump drive and get you the credit card," Marley answered.

"You might as well order ink pens too, and pick up a box to get us through," Lindy was saying to Luna.

"Are you okay on your bike or do you want to take my car?" Marley offered.

"I can fit everything in my saddlebags, but thanks!" She took the jump drive and credit card and left the room.

"Now I'm wondering if there's anything else I forgot to plan for?"

"If anything pops up, we'll handle it as it comes," Marley assured her.

"I know we will. Thanks for helping me achieve this dream."

"Thank you for bringing me and the rest of the team onboard. This is a dream come true for all of us."

†

Their meeting with the caterer went well and plans were set for the grand opening. When they returned to the club, Tom was just leaving.

"I inspected the Roman bath, and have it filling for you. That should wrap us up unless you can think of anything else?"

"No, Tom I think that's the last project to complete. Shoot me over the final invoice tonight and I'll get a payment transferred for you. Thanks for all your hard work to get us up and running ahead of schedule." Lindy shook his hand, and they entered the club. "Let's go check it out."

Pepper and Luna were busy doing client assessments, so she and Lindy were able to sneak past the workout room to check out the bath. The bath was rapidly filling, and Marley could already feel a slight rise in the room temperature. "This is going to be so nice and relaxing."

"Yes, it will. Do you think it will be ready by tonight?" Lindy had a mischievous grin on her face.

"At the rate the water is filling, I'd guess so. I'm assuming it has an automatic shut off when it reaches an appropriate level."

"Indeed, it does," Lindy answered. "Which reminds me, where are we on a maintenance type person?"

"That's the only spot left to fill. I have a few leads, but with everything being new and under warranty, I don't think we have an immediate need. I'd like to wait for the perfect prospect to come along."

"I agree with you there. We've done so well so far staffing the club, I don't feel a necessity to rush."

"I think between Luna's muscle and my semi-handiness we can handle anything small for a while."

"Oh, I'd love to see the two of y'all in tool belts," Lindy smirked.

"Hey now, I'm not just a fantastic set of hands."

"I know you are all that, and so much more," Lindy bumped into her shoulder. "Let's go meet the clients."

†

When they entered the workout area, Marley was introduced to Danna Nichols and Carmen Fultz. Carmen was a beautiful Latino model, perfect body in her early thirties and Danna had more ample curves and was somewhere in her early forties. "I understand we have an appointment for a massage at three when Luna finishes your assessment," Marley said as she shook hands with Danna.

"Yes, we do and I'm so looking forward to it. Lindy raves about your magic hands."

"Lindy is all too kind, but I appreciate the comment. I'll get changed and will have the room ready when you finish here."

"That sounds wonderful. Nice to finally meet you."

"Likewise, Mrs. Nichols."

"Please call me Danna."

Marley nodded and turned to Lindy. "Is there anything else we need to do today?"

"I think we've accomplished plenty. I'm going to stick around and have my assessment done while you're giving Danna a massage."

"I'll see you later then." Marley went into her massage area to prepare the room and then climbed the stairs to her flat. She heard Lindy talking with Luna as she passed by.

"Do you mind if I watch the assessment?"

"Fine with me, if Danna is okay with it," Luna answered.

"I'm sure I don't have anything you haven't seen before," Danna chuckled.

†

Marley had to pinch herself when she got to the flat. This is really happening, and I'm about to provide service to our first official client. She had given thousands of massages, but for some odd reason, she felt butterflies take flight in her stomach. I have no reason to be nervous. Relax, it's just a massage. She opened a fresh bottle of water and took a long drink before heading downstairs. She stopped off at the workout room, just as Luna was finished with the assessment.

Danna looked up at Marley when she entered in shorts and a polo. She felt her eyes appraising her as she approached. "All done here?"

"She's all yours," Luna grinned.

"Do I have time for a quick shower?"

"Of course, do you know where the locker room is?"

"Yes, Luna gave me the complete tour."

"Great, you can slip into one of the robes when you're finished and meet me in room one."

"Thanks. I'll be quick."

Pepper was also nearly finished with her assessment. Carmen looked like she worked out regularly or at least had some awesome body work done. She and Pepper walked over to the group and Carmen looked at Lindy. "Are all services available today?"

Lindy looked at Pepper who nodded. "Yes ma'am, they are."

Pepper led Carmen to the staircase and they disappeared from view.

"One extremely happy client," Luna chuckled.

"Do you have an appointment after our massage?" Marley asked Luna.

"Why yes, Ma'am, I do indeed."

"That should make an interesting pairing," Lindy grinned. "If she doesn't fall down the stairs afterward, why don't you join us in the Roman bath for a refreshing soak?"

"After we run through a quick shower," Luna agreed. "I can't wait to try that out."

"Not spring fed like the originals, but I think it will be passable," Lindy winked at Luna.

Marley smiled at Luna, "I'm going to get ready for Danna. I'll see you all in an hour."

†

Marley put some relaxing music on and took a long drink of water. A few minutes later a light tap on the door let her know Danna had arrived. Marley walked to the entrance. "Come in and take off your robe. Lie face down on the table for me if you would, please."

Danna removed the robe, and Marley hung it behind the door. "Are you having any tightness or sore spots we need to work on?"

"I've been having tension headaches from tightness in my neck."

"I'll see what I can do about relaxing those muscles. Would you mind if I put your hair up in a clip?"

"No problem," she lowered her body onto the massage table.

Marley took a hair clip and gently brushed the long hair away from Danna's neck and secured it on top of her head. "There, all set. Is this music okay for you?"

"It's beautiful. I could fall asleep to that sound."

"Well, be my guest if you want to take a nap."

Danna chuckled. "Don't be surprised if I do."

"What is your impression of the club so far?" Marley asked as she filled her hands with the warmed oil.

"Everything looks fantastic. The staff seems very professional and well equipped to do their jobs. I'm looking forward to working with Luna and Pepper to get into shape. My late husband David wanted me to have some plastic surgery done, but I flatly refused. The good Lord gave me this body, and I need to take better care of how I treat it."

"Were you able to set up your fitness goals?"

"Yes, I'll be working out three to four days a week, getting massages, and working with Pepper on developing better eating habits. I want to be able to drop about thirty pounds."

"That sounds very achievable." Marley started working the warmed oil into Danna's neck and shoulders, kneading the tense muscles deeply. "Let me know if this is too much pressure for you."

"It feels heavenly. It's been ages since I had a massage."

"Don't be surprised if your muscles are sore tomorrow then. Be sure to drink plenty of water tonight and tomorrow to help flush the toxins from your body."

"Thanks, I will."

Marley focused on the massage and felt Danna begin to relax, as she worked her way down her body. She had a good figure and muscle tone. Losing the extra pounds would tighten up her figure and it shouldn't be too difficult for her to achieve her goals. She was happy to hear that she didn't dream of being too thin. Some women became obsessed with weight and did more harm to their bodies than good. When she was working on her hips, she thought she heard a soft moan. "Everything feeling good?"

"Oh yes, Lindy was right, you do have magic hands."

"She's been a regular customer for quite some time, so she would know."

"I hope I'm not being too forward, but do you participate in the upstairs activities as well?"

Marley felt a smile growing on her face. "Yes, I do. All of the staff here except for the front desk woman will be an option for any of our clients. We all have very different techniques, so I hope you will take advantage of the variety of special attention we offer."

Danna's voice was nearly a purr when she answered. "I've always been curious what it would be like with a woman, so rest assured, I will be sampling often."

"I understand you have a special engagement with Luna tonight."

"Yes, I do. I'm very much looking forward to that."

"That is also very good exercise and will help you reach your goals."

"Among other things," Danna chuckled.

"Yes, I guarantee Luna will leave you with a satisfied look on your face tonight."

"I have to admit, it's been a while since I've been satisfied. My husband died from a widow maker heart attack six months ago. Too much red meat and greasy foods. I always told him not to eat so much fried food, but eating was his true love."

"I'm sorry to hear that. Do you have any children?"

"No, David wasn't able to become a father. A low sperm count, or something like that, but he never wanted children anyway."

"Do you want children?"

"I thought I did, but I've gotten used to the idea of being single. I have the luxury to travel anywhere I want to go at any time, so children would complicate that. You never really know what the future may bring though."

"That's right, you could fall in love again and have a house full of kids."

"I don't see that happening, but you never know."

"How are you feeling?"

"Completely relaxed," she answered as Marley massaged her right foot deeply.

"Are you ready to turn over onto your back?"

Danna carefully rolled over. Her green eyes were open as she looked at Marley and even in the dim lighting,

Marley could see how they sparkled with excitement. Marley moved to the end of the table behind Danna's head to continue working on her neck. "Is your neck feeling better?"

"Yes, it feels fantastic."

"That's what I like to hear." Marley smiled down on her. "With regular exercise, massages and improved eating habits, you'll be a new woman before you know it."

"That's what I'm hoping for."

"We'll do our best to make your dreams come true."

Marley's eyes traveled down to Danna's chest and she could see her nipples filled with excitement, as she moved down to her shoulder. "We plan to try out the new Roman bath later tonight if you'd like to join us, after your appointment with Luna."

"I'd like that if I'm able to still walk." Danna smiled. "It's been a while for a lot of things."

"I can understand that." Danna's breasts were firm as her hands glided over them. She could feel her gasp as her hand grazed the edge of a nipple but chose to ignore it and continue down to her abdomen. *I have a feeling she's ready to explode and Luna is just the ignition she needs.* It was hard to hide the smirk on her face as she had that thought. Marley turned her back to Danna for more oil and to allow her to gain control of her senses.

"I'm amazed by how sensual your touch feels. I've had massages before, but this feels different. Much better, but different."

Marley turned back to her. "There's no sexual intent behind my movements, but I try to focus on the erogenous spots that allow the client to relax and feel content, not aroused. I'm not sure if that makes sense to you."

Danna smiled. "It really does. It's been forever since I felt this good. I feel energized and relaxed at the same time."

"That's a perfect description of what I try to accomplish with each massage."

"Sign me up for a lifetime schedule then," Danna chuckled.

"Once, for sure, per week, maybe twice at first will help you continue to relax. Any more than that will not be necessary. As you develop your fitness routine, I think you'll see remarkable changes in how you feel emotionally and how your body feels."

"I can see that already. You ladies are amazing."

"Thank you, I hope we meet your every need. I'm just about done here, but feel free to stay and relax as long as you like." Marley pulled a soft sheet over the front of her body as she worked on the tops of her feet. "I've got a cold bottle of water waiting for you, and I hope you'll drink at least part of it before going upstairs. I'll place it on the table beside you, but please take whatever time you need to relax, then you can put your robe on and meet Luna upstairs in the first flat when you're ready for your next experience."

"Thank you for the lovely massage and making me feel comfortable about being here."

"My pleasure. Do you want me to pencil you in for Tuesday and Thursday next week? Monday is our training day, but we will be fully open for business starting Tuesday."

"Yes, that would be wonderful. Thanks again."

"You're welcome. I hope to see you later in the bath."

Marley dimmed the light further and left the room to give her a few moments to relax. She walked into the workout area to see Luna assessing Lindy's measurements.

"Hey, how'd the massage go?" Luna asked.

"Perfect. She's relaxing and will meet you in the first flat upstairs when she's ready." Marley grinned at Luna. "She's very eager about her appointment with you."

Luna's dark eyes burned with excitement. "I'm just about finished here. I've got the room set up and ready to go."

"I've got to jot down a few notes and set a recurring appointment, so I guess I'll see you later."

"Are we still on for the Roman bath?" Lindy asked.

"I think we all deserve a little relaxing. I'll meet you there in just a few minutes." Marley left the room to wash her hands and spend a few minutes in her office making her notes. She heard Lindy laughing at Luna as she told her, "go ahead, we can finish this later."

Luna raced to catch up with Marley as she walked toward the office. "Any advice on Danna?"

"I can't believe you are asking me for advice. Are you nervous?"

Luna shrugged. "A little bit, I guess. This is my first real appointment."

"I understand, I actually felt nervous about the massage and goodness knows I've done thousands of them. Just relax and be yourself. Go slow and listen to what her body tells you. Your body will do the rest. Have fun and she will too."

Luna hugged her a bit too tightly. "Easy girl," Marley teased. "See you later." She watched Luna race up the steps two at a time and, shaking her head over Luna's exuberance, walked into the office. She sank into the soft leather of her chair and allowed her eyes to close for a moment. It felt good to relax. It had been a long and productive day, but Marley was glad it was almost over. She'd spend some time in the Roman bath with the others and then go upstairs to shower and chill. Her thoughts drifted to the leftover steak in her refrigerator and it made her stomach rumble with anticipation. The noise of her stomach brought her back to reality and she opened her appointment book and set up massages for Danna for the next two weeks. She jotted down a few other notes and shut down the office for the evening.

†

Marley climbed the stairs on the way to her flat to change out of her clothes. She smiled at the sound of pleasure being received in the flat as she crept by the door. Luna was definitely working her magic on Danna. Marley opened the door to her flat and walked to her bedroom to strip out of her clothes. She wrapped the warm robe around her and slipped into a pair of pool sandals, before returning downstairs. The sound level had dramatically increased as she walked past the room and she reminded herself to make sure the sound system was playing music throughout the club when services were being rendered upstairs. As she arrived at the bottom of the stairs, she activated the system with dance music with a rhythmic beat. She was sure Luna would appreciate the prompt from the sound.

She stopped off in her massage room to clean up and store the used sheet. She found a note from Danna, and a fifty-dollar tip thanking her for the session. She tucked the bill into a drawer in a small desk and finished disinfecting her area.

When she arrived at the Roman bath, Lindy was already stripped down and neck deep in the water. "How is the temperature?"

"Not quite at full strength yet, but it still feels terrific. Come join me."

"I'll be on my way in a minute." She stepped out of her sandals and removed her robe, hanging it on a hanger installed on the wall beside Lindy's. She could feel Lindy's eyes on her and when she turned back to the pool, saw the appraising look her employer was giving her. She entered the bath by the shallow steps placed in one of the corners and waded toward Lindy. "You're right, this does feel great."

"I wonder how things are going upstairs?"

"From the sounds coming from the rooms, I'd say they were going quite well." Marley couldn't help but chuckle. "We have to remember to turn the sound system on when we are entertaining upstairs, to keep the sounds from echoing."

"What a delightful problem to have. Speaking of which, may I get a massage and something extra tomorrow night?"

"It would be my pleasure," Marley answered and moaned as she sank down into the water beside Lindy. "What time would you like?"

"We can make it late. Jay Dub will be occupied most of the evening. Six good for you? I know it's after club hours. We could do five if that's better."

"Either will be fine, just let me know. I have a massage appointment with Carmen at three, but nothing yet after."

"Tomorrow sounds like it will be a full day of assessments. I'm sure your schedule will fill up quickly. Luna told me she and Pepper each have ten appointments for tomorrow."

"Wow, that's almost everyone on the list," Marley commented.

"There are a couple out of town at the moment. I told you the women were eager to begin their sessions."

"Yes, you did. I'm glad the rest of the staff will be onboard Monday."

"Will you try to keep the clientele for massages divided up between you and the three other therapists?"

"As much as possible. I think it would be easier to schedule them that way. They can always switch if they aren't delighted with the service."

"I hope you will keep me on your list."

"You're my top priority. Do you still want one massage per week scheduled?"

"For now, let's stick to Fridays. I may occasionally want an extra one, but not routine."

"Just let me know, but I'll block off Friday from five on for you. Does that sound good?"

"Perfect."

Pepper walked in wearing a robe and a huge smile. "Mind if I join you ladies?"

"Not at all. Come on in," Lindy answered. "Is Carmen not joining us?"

"No, she had a dinner scheduled with her family, so she regretfully declined the offer. Maybe next week."

Pepper removed her robe and entered the bath. "Oh, my goodness. This is heavenly."

Lindy smiled up at her, "Yes, it is. It sounds like everyone had a successful day."

"We did, and tomorrow is going to be a full day as well. The clients are eager to get in and started."

"Congratulations, Ladies, on a great unofficial first day."

"Thanks, Boss. It's been a fantastic day," Pepper replied as she lowered her body into the water.

Marley laid her head back against the edge of the bath and closed her eyes.

"Are you tired?" Lindy asked.

"Just relaxing. It's been a productive week."

"We have accomplished more this week than I ever dreamed we could. Would you ladies join me for a celebratory dinner tomorrow night?" Lindy asked.

"I'm pretty sure that can be arranged, especially after a long day tomorrow," Marley said.

"I'll make our reservations at Victor's for eight then," Lindy replied.

Luna and an extremely satisfied looking Danna walked into the bath area. "Are you ready for two more?" Luna asked.

"Absolutely," Marley replied. "The water is fantastic."

With a bashful smile at Luna, Danna turned to Lindy. "Everything here is fantastic. You and the ladies have done a marvelous job."

"I'm so happy you approve. I'm very proud of what we've done so far. Ladies, don't make plans for tomorrow night. I'm taking you three and Hayley if she can join us, out to Victor's for dinner to celebrate a great week."

"You'll get no argument from me, Boss. I've been dying to try that place out for years."

"You can eat to your heart's content then," Lindy chuckled. "I do believe they have a steak that's perfect for you."

"I'll let you corrupt me with red meat for one night." Luna winked.

†

After soaking for another thirty minutes, Lindy suggested they wrap up for the night and head home. After showering, Lindy and Danna left, while Marley, Luna, and Pepper, changed linens in the flats and straightened up the club. When they were all done, Marley walked them to the door. Luna stopped and turned toward her. "How about joining me at Sister's for a little while after dinner tomorrow night? I need to get my groove on the dance floor after all this activity this week. We won't be out long. Pepper and I'll finish the last equipment on Saturday, but we could burn off some steam."

"That sounds like fun. Will you be joining us, Pepper?" Marley asked.

"I'll let you know tomorrow, but it sounds like fun."

"Okay then, I'll see y'all in the morning. Drive safe, Ladies." Marley watched her friends pull out of the parking lot and locked the door behind her and armed the security system before climbing up the stairs. "What a night," she said as she pulled on a pair of sweats and a t-shirt.

She opened the refrigerator to pull out her leftovers and sighed at the emptiness of the unit. "I really must go to the grocery store soon." She took out the last portion of steak and a fresh bottle of water and reheated her dinner.

Marley barely remembered setting her alarm before slipping between her cool sheets and dropping instantly to sleep.

CHAPTER EIGHT

Friday dawned as a beautiful fall day in Atlanta and Marley was eager to get to work after a glass of juice and the last of her yogurts. When Luna arrived early, Marley had made a decision to make a quick grocery run. "Are you okay holding down the fort for a bit while I make a food shopping run?"

"Sure, that's no problem. If we aren't tied up with clients when you get back, we'll help you carry them upstairs."

"Thanks, Luna. My cupboards and fridge are bare. I ate the last of my yogurt this morning."

"Take off then and I'll see you when you return."

"Thanks, I won't take long." Marley walked out the door just as Pepper was arriving. "I'm making a quick trip out but will be back soon. Call me if you need anything."

"Take your time. We've got this covered," Pepper said and entered the building.

†

When she returned an hour later, the parking lot had several new cars she didn't recognize. She walked in with an armful of bags and went straight upstairs. Lindy was waiting for her when she returned and helped her carry the last of the bags upstairs. "You know, I have a service that delivers my groceries to my home and it's well worth the fifteen-dollar charge for the convenience. Why don't I help you get that set up this morning, so all you'll have to do is go online and order?"

"That would be incredible. I detest going to the grocery store, but my supplies were running low."

"You need some help putting these away?"

"No, but thank you. I can get them and I'll meet you back downstairs in just a few minutes."

"Take your time. Pepper and Luna are on a roll. The delivery man called and they will be delivering the last of the equipment in about fifteen minutes. They'll break away from the assessments just long enough to take the delivery, while I entertain the ladies over coffee and juice. Come down and meet them though."

"I'll be there soon," Marley replied, unpacking bags of basic condiments, placing them in the fridge. When she finished, the refrigerator had items on every shelf and the pantry had goods stored as well. Now she was feeling at home. She was smiling as she walked downstairs and nearly collided with a stunning blonde woman.

"Oh, excuse me," she said when she bumped into Marley. "I was looking for the locker room."

"Hi, I'm Marley. Come with me and I'll show you."

"Thanks, I'm Nancy Holcomb. Nice to meet you. Are you the manager and massage therapist Lindy raves about?"

"Yes, that would be me. Nice to meet you as well."

"I'd love to schedule a massage with you."

"I'll get you set up with an appointment today," Marley promised as they entered the locker room. "I'll get my appointment book and meet you in the lounge."

"Perfect," Nancy answered and headed for one of the stalls.

Lindy was sitting around a table, entertaining three other clients, when Marley entered. "Let me grab my appointment book and I'll be right back," she told Lindy after being introduced. "Does anyone need anything while I'm up?"

"No, I think we're good. Pour yourself a coffee or juice when you come back and join us, please."

Marley rushed to her office and picked up her appointment book and those of the other three massage therapists that she had recruited and would be onboard starting Monday. She hoped to have several massages scheduled for them starting on Tuesday. She had already scheduled Danna and Lindy in for several weeks, so she would spread the others out as evenly as possible. With the other duties as manager, she and Lindy had agreed she would limit her sessions to three a day.

She returned to the lounge and poured a glass of apple juice, before joining the ladies at the table. Lindy began to introduce her to Nancy, but Nancy told her they'd already met in a near collision as she was searching for the locker room. "Oh, I'm glad to see you have your appointment book. Can you set me up for Tuesday's and Thursday's at one for the next few weeks?"

Marley opened her appointment book and penciled Nancy as requested, she also explained there were three other therapists beginning Tuesday and booked the other ladies with them. They seemed a bit disappointed about not all being scheduled with Marley, but she assured them the other therapists were just as competent, and if they were not pleased, they could request another therapist.

"We can't overload Marley while the club is still in the opening phases. Maybe as things smooth out, she can take on more if time allows," Lindy added as a consolation.

The delivery men made quick work of bringing in the boxes of equipment and when they were gone, Luna came to take the two ladies whose assessments were interrupted by the delivery and told the other two that they'd be with them shortly.

"This place is amazing, Lindy," Sharon said. "I'm so glad you came up with this idea. It makes perfect sense. Robert is dying to know more. I told him it's a ladies' only facility, and no men, even husbands were allowed."

"Several of the women have told me that they are getting questions from their husbands," Lindy said. "They've had their fun for all these years and now it's our turn."

"Amen to that," Mel, one of the clients said, in agreement. "And it's about damn time."

†

The afternoon passed quickly and Marley was preparing for Carmen's massage when Lindy walked into the room. "Can we do my massage when you finish with Carmen? That way I can get home, shower and dress in time for our dinner reservation."

"We still on for something extra afterward?"

"Oh, most definitely."

"Good, I'm taking over flat number five, it's next door to mine and will make it more convenient. I have something special planned for you tonight."

Lindy grinned with excitement. "Do I need to go home for a change of clothes now?"

"That might not be a bad idea," Marley smiled with her response.

"I'll see you at four then." Lindy left the room as Luna came in to prop in the doorway.

"What on earth did you say to her? She ran out of here like a scalded cat."

"She's going home for a change of clothes, so she can shower and we'll leave for dinner from here. Why don't you plan on riding with me and you can stay here after we get back from Sister's later?"

"That's not a bad idea. I'll be back before you finish with Carmen. We've got something extra planned for afterward."

"High five," Marley said and slapped Luna's palm. "I'll be sure and get her well-oiled for you," she laughed.

"Going to be the ride of her life. See ya in a bit."

"Be careful and keep your eyes on the road."

"Yes, Mom," Luna shouted back and left the club.

Moments later, the door opened and Carmen arrived for her massage. "I saw Luna leaving. I hope she's coming back." Her face turned into a frown.

"She just had to run home for a few minutes. She'll be back before your session is finished."

"Oh, thank goodness. That had me worried for a minute."

"She is very much looking forward to your appointment." Marley watched the smile return to Carmen's face. "Are you ready for your massage?"

"I am so ready."

"I'll give you a few minutes to undress and you can lie face down and pull the sheet over you if that makes you comfortable. I'll knock to see if you're ready."

"Thank you," she said and closed the door behind her.

Marley walked to the lounge to retrieve two bottles of water and then knocked. She heard Carmen say, "Come in," and slipped through the door.

"Is this music and lighting okay for you?"

"Yes, thanks, it's very soothing."

"Alright, then we'll get started. Are there any tender or sore spots I need to be aware of before I begin?"

"My lower back has been feeling tight lately."

"I'll see if I can't loosen those muscles up a bit. Let me know if the pressure gets too intense."

Marley began working the muscles in Carmen's neck and shoulders, rubbing the fragrant oil deep into her skin. "Oh, that feels so nice," she whispered softly. Marley smiled, thinking *you haven't felt nice until Luna works her magic.* She was thinking this to herself but felt a growing smile on her face. "It only gets better from here," she promised.

"That sounds intriguing," Carmen purred.

Marley kneaded her lower back, loosening the tightness and she could feel Carmen relax beneath her hands. "Is that feeling better?"

"I haven't felt this relaxed in ages."

"Good, I'll move on then." Marley continued working her way down Carmen's lean legs, working the oil smoothly across her skin and when she reached for her left foot, Carmen giggled.

"I'm sorry, but I'm a bit ticklish."

"That's no problem." Marley finished her feet and asked her to roll over. She noted how erect her nipples had grown and wondered if she had plastic surgery to enhance her breast size. Regardless, they were perfectly shaped firm mounds that she knew Luna would be enjoying rather soon. She couldn't help but think of how Luna would please this beautiful young woman and she tried to clear the thoughts from her head to concentrate on her massage. She worked her way down the front of Carmen's body. "Still feeling good?"

"Good doesn't begin to describe how I feel."

Marley smiled. As she worked down the insides of Carmen's thighs, she could feel the heat radiating off her center. She was definitely a hot body now. *Get a grip girl*, she chastised herself. As she was finishing up the massage, she asked, "Do you know where to meet Luna?"

"She said she'd be waiting for me in flat number one."

"That's correct. There's a robe behind the door you can slip on and take your clothes upstairs. Take whatever time you need to relax and try to drink a bit of the water I've left beside you."

"Thank you so much. I feel so much better now thanks to you."

"My pleasure. I'll see you next week. Enjoy your time with Luna." Marley slipped quietly through the door, carrying her water bottle and walked to her office after washing her hands. She was surprised to find Lindy there waiting for her. "Carmen is just finishing up in room one, but we can use another room if you want to get started."

"I can wait a few more minutes to give you time. No need to mess up another room. I doubt it will take Carmen long to get upstairs."

"I know that's right. Give me a minute to prepare the room and I'll be ready."

"Thanks, Marley."

✝

Marley returned to find the room empty and another fifty-dollar tip on the table next to the folded sheet. "I can get so used to this." She wiped down the table and changed the music to something Lindy enjoyed. She turned on an aromatic burner with her favorite scent and was setting up a bottle of water for Lindy when she entered in a robe and closed the door.

"I turned on the sound system upstairs."

"I'm glad you remembered. Once we open next week, I think we should program the system upstairs to come on at a particular time."

"That's a great idea."

"Ready?"

"Always ready for those hands of yours." Lindy hung the robe behind the door and lay face down on the table."

"Any special requests today?"

"More attention to my shoulders. They've been aching lately."

"I'll give them some extra treatment. You just relax and leave the driving to me."

"Yes, Ma'am," Lindy answered with laughter in her voice.

Marley went to work on Lindy's body and mentally practiced the special surprise she had in store for her afterward. She wanted to spice things up a bit for her and she hoped Lindy would approve. When she finished the massage, she handed Lindy her robe. "I'll clean up here and meet you in flat five in just a few minutes. Drink some water while you're waiting."

"See you soon." Lindy smiled and left the room.

Marley prepared the room for the next client and turned off the equipment before heading upstairs. She opened the door to find Lindy sitting naked on the side of the bed. "I want to try something different with you tonight and I hope that you'll trust me," she said as she walked over to the bed and opened a drawer to take out a black blindfold. She saw Lindy's eyebrows shoot upward.

"Well, this is certainly an interesting start. I trust you completely."

"Good," Marley whispered as she placed the blindfold over Lindy's eyes. "Relax back on the bed while I go change. I'll be right back."

Marley waited until Lindy was comfortable and then slipped into her flat to undress. She slipped a robe over her body and walked to the kitchen. She opened up the refrigerator and removed a tray and a few other chilled items. She kicked the door closed and returned to the flat next door. She set the tray beside the table and sat down next to Lindy. "You look good enough to eat."

"You say the sweetest things," Lindy chuckled.

"Will you move over in the bed just a little please?" She waited until Lindy had repositioned and then carefully placed the tray within reach on the bed. She slipped out of her robe and straddled Lindy's legs on the bed.

"That's a nice spot for you."

"I'm so looking forward to our dinner tonight, but I thought I'd have you as an appetizer."

"Oh my, I do love the sound of that. You know about those signs on Chinese buffets, right? Take all you want, but eat all you take," she chuckled.

"Oh, I plan to do just that," Marley answered, with a voice husky with desire. She leaned forward and teased Lindy's lips with a few kisses. "I'm starving."

Marley raised back up and reached for a bottle of chocolate syrup and flipped the cap open. She looked down to see Lindy's nipples perked in anticipation. She raised the bottle slightly above Lindy's chest and began drizzling the chocolate in swirls on her breast and when she reached the nipple, she coated it completely. She felt Lindy's hips lurch, when the cold syrup made contact, with her heated skin. "With any masterpiece, you have to start with a good foundation," she whispered, as she moved to repeat the sequence on her other breast. She drew a line of chocolate between her cleavage down to her navel and filled her navel with the chilled syrup.

"You are such a tease, Marley," Lindy whispered.

"Should I stop?"

"No ma'am, I'd hate to ruin your masterpiece."

Marley capped the syrup and returned it to the tray and picked up a pineapple ring and placed it surrounding Lindy's right nipple.

"I smell pineapple," she said.

"You are so right," Marley answered. She completed layering the second ring and returned to the tray for a can of whipped topping. She filled the space between the ring and Lindy's nipple with the topping, making her giggle with the sound of the can discharging. Then she opened a jar of maraschino cherries and pulled one out by the stem, coating her fingertips in the savory juice. She traced Lindy's lips with the juice and her tongue snaked out for a taste.

"Umm, cherries."

"I have a challenge for you."

"That would be what, my dear?"

Marley dangled the cherry in front of Lindy's lips. "Since your tongue likes to be involved, if you can tie this cherry stem into a knot, I will reward you with a very special treat." Lindy opened her mouth to respond, and Marley placed the cherry on her lips.

Lindy took the cherry into her mouth, devouring the cherry. Marley could see her mouth moving as she concentrated on tying a knot. She smiled and widened the line of chocolate running down the front of Lindy, and then placed twelve halved strawberries in the line of chocolate. Lindy was starting to wiggle beneath her and she warned, "Be still or you'll ruin my masterpiece." Lindy went still as Marley moved further down her body. She took her leisure, lapping the chocolate from Lindy's navel, the tip of her tongue lapping at the sweet syrup. She flatted out her tongue licking up her skin until she reached the first strawberry, and as her teeth bit into it, the juice dripped onto her skin. Lindy moaned at the sensation of Marley's hot tongue sliding down her side as she captured the escaping juice.

"I'm not sure how much more of that I can take."

"You'll take it all," Marley answered, as she moved further up Lindy's body, devouring the chocolate and strawberries until she was once more straddling Lindy's legs. She could see the rise and fall of Lindy's chest, as her breathing grew shallow as her anticipation increased. Marley licked slow circles around her breasts, removing the thick chocolate and then began to nibble the cherries, the tip of her tongue flicking across Lindy's nipple as she ate each cherry and pineapple ring. "How are you doing with that cherry stem?"

"Almost there," Lindy groaned, as Marley's hot mouth covered her left breast, sucking it deeply into her mouth.

"Good," she replied as her mouth and tongue trailed across to her right breast to remove the sweet treats.

"Got it," she said triumphantly with the stem clenched between her teeth.

Marley leaned up to take the stem from her mouth and tossed it onto the tray. She covered her mouth with a feverish kiss and could feel Lindy's body arching upward, to make contact with hers. "Are you ready for your reward?"

"Oh, yes please Marley. I'm soaking wet waiting for you," she answered with a breathy voice.

"Spread your legs," she instructed, and Marley opened her thighs.

Marley reached down between them and entered her with two fingers, sliding deeply inside, as her hips arched to meet them. "Very nice," she whispered against Lindy's cheek, and then moved down her body, her fingers sliding between her soaked and clenching lips. Marley could feel the inner muscles as they clamped around her fingers as she drove deeper inside. Her hot breath burned a trail of desire down Lindy's as her tongue flattened to remove the last of the sticky chocolate. Lindy's hips arched powerfully with every thrust of her fingers and she began gasping for air. "Not yet," she breathed against her skin as her fingers slowed to a stop and curled inside her warmth. Marley reached across with her left hand to remove a cube of ice and placed it in her mouth. Her fingers resumed moving inside and her hand covered a breast and began teasing Lindy's nipple. Marley's head lowered and her mouth covered Lindy's clit, sending the sensation of cold and heat into her most sensitive spot as she added a third finger thrusting between her pulsing lips.

"Oh, hell yes," Lindy cried out, as Marley trapped her clit inside her mouth, sucking it hard as Lindy's body exploded in pleasure, her hips bucking wildly into Marley's face as her body gushed juices onto the bed. Marley lifted her face to crunch the remaining ice, and slowly removed her fingers from Lindy. Lindy's hands still clenched the sheets as Marley lay atop her and covered her mouth, sharing the sweetness of the syrup and fruit, and the taste of her passion with Lindy. Her hand softly caressed her face, then she rolled beside Lindy to allow her to regain her breath. She gently removed the blindfold as a tear slid from the corner of Lindy's eye. Marley wiped the tear with a fingertip and looked into Lindy's eyes.

"That was beyond fantastic," Lindy whispered as she ran her fingertips down Marley's face. "I've never felt so amazing before. I'll gladly volunteer to be your appetizer any time," she said with a chuckle.

Marley pulled her into her arms and held her for several long minutes, not saying a word as none were needed. The joy she saw on Lindy's face told her how much she enjoyed the experience. "Do you need some water?"

"Yes, please."

Marley sat up on the bed and reached for a bottle of water she handed to Lindy, then removed the tray from the bed, placing it on the table. "We both need a shower," she grinned, as she wiped the sticky chocolate from her chest.

"Yes, but not together, or we will be terribly late for our dinner," Lindy chuckled. "Thank you again for such a beautiful experience."

Marley returned her smile. "I'll meet you downstairs in just a bit then," Marley said and slipped the robe over her body and took the tray into her flat.

†

Marley finished dressing after a long, relaxing shower to find Luna waiting for her in the lounge, looking refreshed and ready to party. "Has Lindy come down yet?"

"About ten minutes ago. She looked very satisfied I might add."

"How'd your adventure go with Carmen?"

Lune grinned. "She's a handful of hot loving. She nearly wore me out changing several positions."

"Wait, stop right there, we're drifting in too much information land," Marley teased.

"Sorry, Boss. It was a great workout. How about we leave it at that?"

"That's perfect. Let me grab my keys from the office and we can get on the road. I'm starved."

"Amen to that. I feel like I could eat a whole steer."

Marley walked to the office and found a note from Lindy and three hundred-dollar bills. She slipped one of them into her pocket and placed the other two in her desk. Luna was finishing off a bottle of water when she returned. "Ready to ride?"

"Right behind you. I'll lock up."

Marley walked to her car and waited for Luna. When she climbed inside, Luna said, "You know, I was thinking of saving up some money and buying a Jeep. I love my bike, but it's not always a convenient mode of transportation."

She smiled at her friend. "I was thinking I might trade old Betsy in too. She's been so reliable I hate to let her go. I may hand her down to my oldest nephew who will be old enough to drive soon, to keep her in the family."

"I'm sure he'd appreciate that. My first vehicle was a seventies-era Ford truck, and I drove her until her wheels were about to fall off."

"This old girl was my first brand new car. I drove mom's Impala after she died, until I started having problems with it, and decided to go new."

"At the rate these ladies are going, we could both probably buy new soon." Luna smiled. "There's nothing better than to get compensated well for the things you love most."

"I'll agree with you there." Marley pulled out of the parking lot as something triggered a memory. "I believe Danna's deceased husband owned a string of car dealerships. Maybe she can work you into a nice Jeep deal."

"There's a thought. I'll bring it up to her in the future after I have some money put back." She rolled the window down for fresh air and to let the wind blow through her hair.

"I'm ready for a night on the dance floor at Sister's. I can't believe it's been over a week since I've been there."

"You and Pepper have been very busy this week getting the equipment set up. How long do you think it will take you to finish tomorrow?"

"No more than a couple of hours. Why, do you have something planned?"

"I thought I might cook breakfast in the morning and after you finish setting up the equipment, you can help me set up a workout routine."

"I'd love that. I'll even volunteer to cook breakfast if you'd like," Luna offered.

"Your omelet was very tasty last time."

"Do you have all the ingredients?"

"Yes ma'am, I do. Lindy set me up with a grocery delivery service today and I think I'll go online while y'all are working and put in a major order to get me well stocked. I got some very basic items today."

"That sounds like a good idea. Would you mind if I cook in your flat? After we both sleep in for a bit."

"You're welcome to cook, but I don't think my body understands the whole sleeping in concept anymore. I'll enjoy my coffee and maybe order my groceries if I'm awake before you."

"That works for me."

†

When they arrived at Victor's, Pepper and Haley were just getting out of their car. "Hey, it's good to see you," Marley said as she hugged Haley's neck. "I hope you're ready for work Monday."

"I am so ready. I finished out my notice at my other job, and I'm excited about a new adventure. From the stories Pepper is bringing home, it's turning into a great place."

"It's been a busy week and I'm looking forward to you coming onboard to help with some of the office work. Appointments alone will keep you busy."

"Awesome, I like busy. Do you think the coffee and juice bar will be used a lot?"

"I think it's rapidly turning into a hangout spot," Luna stated.

"We've accumulated some laundry already, but I'll get everything laundered tomorrow," Marley said.

"Don't worry about it. I was planning to come with Pepper tomorrow, so I can do it while they finish setting up the equipment." Haley smiled. "It gives me a great reason to come out and set up my work area too."

"Fine by me. Let's go eat ladies," Marley directed them to the front door.

†

Lindy's face was beaming as her guests arrived. Luna nearly drooled over the menu and Lindy encouraged her to select the porterhouse steak. "If you're going to be corrupted, you might as well make it worth the trip."

"I'll take you up on that, Boss, I'm starving," Luna answered with a smile.

"You have all worked hard this week, and deserve a great hot meal," Lindy looked at Haley. "Don't worry, your hard work starts next week."

Haley smiled back at her. "I'm ready to be a part of this."

Lindy looked at her staff around the table. "After Monday's orientation, it's going to be full swing at the club,

106

so enjoy this relaxing meal. It may be your last for a while," she said with a wicked grin.

The food and wine were delicious and when they finished eating around ten, Lindy left the group in the parking lot. "I'll see you all Monday. Have a great weekend."

"You too, Boss," Luna and Marley said in unison, followed by a laugh.

Luna turned to Pepper and Haley. "We're going to Sister's for a visit if y'all want to come."

"Thanks," Pepper said. "I think we're going to enjoy a quiet evening at home. Have a good time. You both have earned it this week."

"Amen to that sista," Luna said. "Drive careful and I'll see you around ten. Is that good for y'all?"

"Wonderful. See you then." Pepper opened the car door for Haley.

Luna turned to Marley with a wide smile. "Let's party!"

They climbed inside Marley's car and she started the ignition, then turned to Luna. "You realize if you pick someone up tonight, you have to make it back to your place, right?"

Chuckling, Luna said, "Tonight is not one of those nights. I've had such a great sexual workout this week, I just want to dance and have some fun."

"I know, but I also know how Luna madness sets in when you start dancing, and the ladies go wild for you."

"No worries, Boss. I understand the importance of discretion for all of us. I wouldn't dare screw up such a good thing with my libido."

"I understand." Marley put the car in drive and they headed for Sister's. At nearly eleven on a Friday night, the club would be packed. They had to drive two blocks down to find a parking spot. The beat from the club was thumping and greeted them each time the door opened. The upstairs porches were filled with women and several whistled catcalls when they saw them approach. "Bout damn time you got here Luna," someone called from the crowd.

"It sounds like my kinda night," Luna said as they walked up the front steps.

A young blonde met Luna at the front entrance and pulled her straight to the dance floor, leaving Marley laughing in their wake. She wove through the crowd to take the only remaining seat at the bar. Chancy, a blue spiked haired bartender caught her eye and motioned to her she'd be right over. Marley nodded and surveyed the crowd. Luna was a kid in a candy shop inside these walls.

"Hey stranger, what can I get you?"

"Hi, Chancy, how about a cold Corona?"

"With lime?"

"Is there any other way?"

"I'll be right back."

Chancy returned with a bottle of Corona with a wedge of lime stuck in the neck. "Where have the two of y'all been?"

"Working our tails off."

"I hear that. It's good to see y'all again. Start you a tab?"

"Yes please."

Before Chancy had time to move, a sultry voice called out from behind Marley. "Where do you want these?"

"Place them over by the cooler please, Alex," Chancy replied. "Bring several more when you can."

"You got it," the woman said as she walked past Marley carrying several cases of beer.

Marley only caught a glimpse of the short cropped black hair and the tight ass in blue jeans as they passed by and turned back to find Chancy watching her.

"That's Alex. She arrived on our doorstep a couple of days ago, asking for work. She's not much of a conversationalist, but she's a hard worker and the ladies seem to enjoy the view," Chancy chuckled. "Janice and Selene met with her and agreed to let her work for Sister's until she can get her feet under her. She can fix virtually everything and saved us a ton by repairing some of the upstairs plumbing for us. We use her for a bar back during club hours to bring out cases of beer and supplies. From somewhere out west, I think she said. She's staying in the small apartment upstairs, for now."

Alex placed the cases of beer on the floor and turned back toward Marley. She felt herself swallow hard when her eyes made contact with Alex's. Smoldering was the first thought that jumped into her mind, looking at the dark, nearly black eyes of the handsome Hispanic woman. It probably wouldn't be hard for her to be confused for a male, but those eyes were definitely an attraction in themselves. Marley tore her eyes away and looked back to Chancy feeling flushed.

"Yeah, she gets that reaction a lot." Chancy chuckled and walked away.

Marley pushed the lime into the bottle and took a long drink. Alex smiled as she passed by and Marley returned her smile. *Holy shit. The ladies at TWC would go wild over that look. Who am I kidding, she is a hottie in a very different way.* She couldn't help but admire the flex of the muscles in her arms as she returned carrying three more cases of beer. *I wonder what her story is?*

After ten minutes on the dance floor, the lights flickered to indicate the drag show was about to begin. Marley watched Luna separate herself from a throng of women and approach the bar. She squeezed onto a seat vacated by a woman who moved closer to the stage to view the show. A light coating of sweat beaded across Luna's forehead.

"Man, it's hot out there," she said as she wiped her brow. She nodded to Chancy who reached into the cooler for a bottle of water and headed their way.

"I'm glad someone finally let you out of the house," she said with a wink to Luna.

"You wouldn't believe how hard we've been working," Luna told Chancy.

"Uh huh, that's the story Marley told me, too."

Luna grinned at Marley. "That's our story, and we're sticking to it."

"Holla at me when you're ready for a fresh beer," she said to Marley, then moved on to serve another customer.

"You ought to see the new hottie they have working as a bar back," Marley said.

"You think someone's a hottie? This I have to see," Luna teased.

"Hey, I think several women are hotties, present company included."

Luna nearly choked on the drink of water she had just gulped. "What did you just say? Did I hear you infer that I was a hottie?"

"Yes, but don't let it go to your head."

"You've never told me that before."

Marley blushed. "I reckon it just slipped out by accident."

"Thank you. That makes my night. Hmmm, I think I know who you're referring to now," she was looking over Marley's head to the backroom entrance. "Androgynous, Hispanic type?"

"That would be the one. Chancy says her name is Alex. Came in a few days ago with one of her regulars and stepped in to fix a leaking tap for them and eager to let them know she was looking for work. Chancy said she's a great bar back and can fix virtually anything." Marley watched Luna's face as she continued. "She's staying in the apartment above the bar until she can get on her feet."

"She's definitely got the looks, and it sounds like she's handy with tools. Of all kinds, I bet." Luna wiggled her eyebrows, causing Marley to laugh. "Should we ask to meet with her later?"

"I'd hate to steal good help from Sister's, but yeah, I'd like to at least chat with her for a bit."

Janice, one of the owners of Sister's interrupted their conversation and Marley wondered if she'd somehow overheard them talking about her new employee.

"Hey Marley, Luna. I see you've noticed Alex. She's something, huh?" Janice said.

"How about an introduction?" Marley asked.

Janice laughed. "Get in line. You wouldn't believe the women who want to catch her eye, but for you, sure, I'll take you over to meet her."

After Janice had introduced Luna and her to Alex, it was clear that she was a bit territorial about Alex. They'd had a short interchange and Janice had made it clear she wouldn't be happy if Marley tried to poach her. She was almost going to give the whole idea up when Luna suggested she talk with Alex while she was away from her boss and fixing the broken toilet.

"Let me sneak into the bathroom and see if she's interested while she's fixing their broken toilet. Maybe she just said that about being loyal and happy here because Janice was standing right there. I'll be right back. Why don't you let me go solo with her until we can find out a bit more about her past? She just hit town, so let me dig into more of her backstory."

Marley considered Luna's idea. It probably was a good idea to find out more about the curious woman. She could be an ax murderer running from the FBI for all she knew. She couldn't let her hormones get the best of her and lead her into something that would be dangerous for the club. There was too much invested for everyone. She took a long drink and watched Luna approach Alex. She nodded at Luna, and the two handsome women disappeared into the main bathroom.

†

Luna approached Alex while she had her hands in the back of the tank. "Hey, you mind if I steal a few minutes of your time?"

Alex turned around and nodded. "Sure, as long as you don't mind me continuing to fix this."

"Thanks, I'm a personal fitness trainer and we've just opened up a new club. We are looking for someone handy with tools. I'm not suggesting you give up your job at Sister's, but maybe you could re-consider working at both places. Chancy told me that you were great with general maintenance and a hard worker. Do you mind if I ask for some background information? Experience? Commitment to stay in the Atlanta area, etc.?"

"Sure. I grew up in Texas and spent a little time in Nevada. I worked with my dad in the family business until he made a bad hiring decision and his handyman service got shut down." Alex paused for a few seconds. "I'm not sure I should tell you everything, but I might not have all the papers necessary to work for you."

Luna nodded and considered the ramifications of what Alex had just shared. She could read between the lines and assumed Alex was undocumented. "What were you doing in Nevada?"

"I found employment at a place called Sheri's Ranch. I thought it was one of those fancy resorts in Vegas and I thought I could get on doing housekeeping. To make this a shorter story, I wasn't officially hired, but one of the ladies who worked in the bordello took me under her wing and gave me a place to stay. She taught me the tricks of the trade, and I specialized in Nuru massages for female clients. Things didn't quite work out there and I headed East."

Luna was leaning forward, listening intently to her story. "What happened?"

"I was getting ready to give a massage when the client's abusive husband busted in and started whaling on her. I think my mind snapped for a few seconds, and the fat bastard ended up with a broken nose, and some chipped teeth. He left the room, screaming about calling the law for assault, even though he was the one doing the assaulting."

"Did you get arrested?"

"I didn't stick around. When I went to my friend Ariel and told her what happened, she drove me home. I didn't want to cause any trouble for Sheri's, so I asked her to drive me out of town, and I managed to get a ride to Atlanta from a sweetheart of a trucker."

"Wow, that is quite a story. What are your intentions for staying in Atlanta?"

"I'd like to settle down here. I think if the law was after me, they would have tracked me down by now. I think the fat bastard was too embarrassed to report he got his ass kicked by a woman to be honest, but I couldn't jeopardize the ranch after all they'd done for me."

Luna smiled. "I can certainly appreciate that. Tell me a little more about your skills."

"There's not much about plumbing or electricity I can't manage. Painting, drywall, concrete, you name it, I've done it. Unfortunately, I'm not licensed, but can still perform the work to perfection."

"Is there anyone at Sheri's that could vouch for you or give you a reference?"

"Ariel, I assume of course, but the Human Resource Department couldn't since I wasn't actually on their books. They might, or might not even confirm who I am, if it may jeopardize their status."

"Are you planning to stay here for long? Is there a number I can reach you?"

"I don't have a cell, but I'm living upstairs and you can always find me here at Sister's. Other than going out and about a little here and there, I stay pretty close to the bar."

"I come here often, so I'm sure we can connect again. Think about things in the meantime and maybe we can see if something will work out for both of us."

"Okay. I better finish up here. Sorry to cut things short, but I have a reputation to maintain and I'm usually pretty fast at fixing things. Can I ask you a question?"

"Sure."

"Are you with the attractive woman sitting at the end of the bar?"

"That is Marley, your potential boss, so play nice," Luna grinned. "Speaking of Marley, I better get back to her. She'll want a play by play on our conversation."

"Okay, I'll see you in a few minutes. Thanks, Luna."

"You're very welcome." Luna exited the bathroom and returned to the bar. She was able to claim the seat beside Marley.

"Well?"

"Very interesting, but we need to talk later, okay?" Luna replied. She noticed the show was ending. "Was it a short show or was I gone longer than I thought?"

"You were gone long enough for me to finish my beer." She was getting ready to catch Chancy's attention to signal for a fresh one when Alex returned to the bar and smiled at her. When she saw Marley's empty bottle, she reached out her hand. "Let me replace that for you."

"Thanks," Marley handed her the bottle.

She turned to find Luna watching her with interest. "Should I be jealous?"

"You have to admit, she's not hard on the eyes if you are into the androgynous type."

"Which you seem to be."

"I appreciate a good body, quick smile and passionate eyes."

Luna grinned, "We can continue this exploration of your favorite body types later. Right now, you need to dance with me."

Marley laughed at her comment and allowed Luna to lead her to the dance floor. Just as they arrived, the frantic dance beat ended and a slow, love song began to play. *Oh great, I get to be pressed up close to the hottest body in here. Eat your heart out, Ladies.* She imagined eyes like daggers boring into her back right now, as a dozen or more ladies would die to be in Luna's arms.

Luna's eyes sparkled with excitement as she spun Marley around, and pulled her close. The cologne she wore, blended well with her body heat and chemistry. Marley found herself feeling lightheaded for a moment. She leaned into Luna's body for support. When their bodies made contact, Marley felt a shiver from deep within. Their bodies molded together in a perfect fit and Marley felt herself melting into Luna as they moved across the dance floor. The heat between their bodies was almost unbearable and ignited her soul. *Damn, I want this woman.* Her nipples were so erect, it was almost painful and Marley wondered if Luna could feel them pressed into her skin. *Why am I thinking these things right now?*

Luna was an excellent dancer and easily led her across the dance floor. She was careful not to allow her hands to wander over Marley, as they were often prone to do with a dance partner. She felt Marley's body quivering and looked down into her eyes. "You cold?"

"No, I'm okay, was just feeling a little lightheaded."

"You want to go home?"

Marley shook her head and leaned in closer to Luna. "Your body feels warm. Are you sure you're not running a fever?" Luna's hand caressed Marley's forehead. "You're hot and you're starting to sweat. Come on, I'm taking you home." She cut their dance short and handed Chancy a twenty and the fresh Corona to Alex. "She's not feeling well, so we're going to call it a night."

"Thanks," Alex replied and watched them leave the club.

When they stepped outside, the cooler air did little to refresh Marley. She dug her keys out of her pocket and handed them to Luna. "Would you mind driving? I'm feeling a bit nauseated."

"No problem." Luna raced ahead to open the car door for Marley. "Do you think it was something you ate?"

"I hope not. That meal was perfect the first time. I bet the second time wouldn't be near as nice."

"Let's get you home and settled. Do you have anything for nausea or do we need to stop for something?"

"I'm pretty sure I have something in my medicine cabinet. Just get me home, and hopefully, I can sleep this off."

Luna jogged around the car and slipped in behind the wheel. She started the engine and turned when she heard Marley lower the window for fresh air. "You okay?"

"Yeah, I think so. I'll let you know if I need you to pull over."

"Hang on and I'll get you home as fast as I can." Luna shifted into gear and reached over to place her hand on Marley's shoulder. She could feel the heat rising up to meet her. *This is not good.*

Luna had nearly made it back to the club when Marley cried out, "Pull over." Thankfully traffic was light and she pulled off the road immediately. Marley flung the door open and staggered out two steps before losing the contents of her stomach. Luna put the car in gear and searched the console until she found a few napkins. She grabbed her bottle of water and raced around the car.

"You okay?" She wet one of the napkins with the cool water and handed it to Marley to wipe her mouth.

"Thanks. Sorry about that."

"No need to apologize. Wipe your face and then take a small sip of water to rinse your mouth. It wouldn't hurt you to drink a little bit either, tiny sips though."

Marley nodded and took the water, rinsing her mouth and spitting the vile tasting liquid into the grass. Then she leaned back into the car and took a small drink. "That's so much better. Thank you."

"No problem. Can you handle a few more minutes until we get home?"

"Yes, I don't think I have anything left." Marley allowed Luna to guide her into the car and secure her seatbelt.

Luna deactivated the alarm and then set it once they were inside. She helped Marley up the stairs to her flat. "Are you up to taking a shower after you get some anti-nausea meds and some Tylenol in you?"

"Yeah, I think I need one now."

"If you'll take the medicine, I'll make you a slice of toast or a bagel to help soak up some of the acids in your stomach. I know you bought bagels. Is that good?"

"Probably a good idea, with some water. Thanks for taking care of me Luna."

"That's what friends are for," she used Marley's keys to open the flat. "I'll give you a few minutes after I hear the shower running to make your bagel but call me if you need help."

"Thanks," Marley made her way into her bedroom for a t-shirt and panties before walking into the bathroom. "Water to one hundred twelve," she instructed and slipped out of her clothes, tossing them into the hamper. She dug through the medicine cabinet until she found what she needed and swallowed the pills. Then she brushed her teeth. When she stepped into the shower, she couldn't help but moan at the feel of the water against her skin.

Luna heard the shower running and walked to the kitchen to find the bag of bagels and some softened butter. She checked to make sure there was plenty of cold bottled water and dropped the bagel in the toaster. She leaned against the counter while she waited on the toaster. Marley's reaction to Alex's physical appearance had surprised her. She felt a pang of jealousy at the way her eyes had devoured Alex's body. Other than being a bit taller than Alex, they had pretty much the same build, but Marley never looked at her like that. Or did she? She had never noticed such a visceral reaction from Marley. The bagel popped in the toaster and the sound made her jump. She laughed at being startled back to reality. Luna heard the water shut off and the shower door open. She smiled as she spread a light coating of butter over the toasted bread and took out a bottle of water. She placed the bottle beside the bed and turned to see Marley walking toward her in an oversized t-shirt, and her hair still damp from the shower. She felt her heart flutter. "How are you feeling?" She felt the quiver in her voice and hoped Marley didn't catch it.

"Much better. Thanks."

"Come have a seat on the bed and I'll get your bagel." She twisted the cap off the water and handed it to her. "Go slow."

"Yes, Mom." Marley smiled and took the bottle of water.

"I know you're probably tempted to guzzle it but start with small sips."

"I do feel like a sponge. I'll take it easy though."

Marley took a seat and was watching Luna when she turned back around. Her smile was brilliant for someone who had been physically ill just minutes ago. "I'm glad you're feeling better." Luna handed her the plate holding the toasted bagel.

"Will you share it with me?" Marley took the plate and offered the other half to Luna.

"It does look good."

"Come sit with me." Marley tucked her legs under the covers and patted the bed beside her.

Luna sat on the edge of the bed and took a bite. "This is good. If your stomach is up to it, I'll cook a nice breakfast for you in the morning."

"I'm looking forward to one of your omelets. I'm sorry we had to cut the night short. I know you were looking forward to a night of dancing. I feel bad that I took you away from the fun, but thank you for taking care of me."

"No problem. Besides, I got the dance I wanted." She winked and relaxed back onto the bed. "Do you realize that's the first dance we've ever shared?"

"Seriously?"

"Yes, seriously and we've known each other for a few years."

Marley smirked. "You're usually swarmed by women who want to dance with you once you hit the club."

"Sometimes. Thank you for dancing with me."

"It was my pleasure. You're a great dancer."

"It's something that comes easily to me. Like breathing."

"I wish it came that easy to me. I feel like I flounder like a fish out of water. All spasmodic and stuff."

Luna couldn't hold back her laughter. "I can assure you that you aren't spasmodic. You just need to relax and let the music take you."

Marley swallowed the last bite of her bagel. "Maybe you could give me some lessons?"

"I'd love to, but right now you need to get some sleep. I'll stay with you until you fall asleep if that's okay."

"I'm sure I'll be fine. You need to get some rest too."

"I will." Luna stood and waited for Marley to slide down the bed and pulled the covers over her. "Sleep and I'll see you in a few hours." She watched Marley close her eyes and turned off the bedside lamp, leaving the room lit only by the bathroom light. She walked over to a small bench at the end of the bed and sat down to watch her friend sleep. Even in the dim light, she could see the relaxed smile on Marley's face. So beautiful.

†

Two hours later, Marley awoke to find Luna slumped over on the bench sleeping. She climbed down the end of the bed and gently shook her awake. "Hey, sleepyhead."

Luna startled from her touch, "I guess I fell asleep." She stretched. "I wanted to make sure you were okay before I left."

"You don't have to go to another flat, but you do have to at least get comfortable." Marley patted the bed beside her.

Luna wiped her hair out of her face and kicked her shoes off. She walked around the side of the bed and slipped between the sheets. "How are you feeling?"

"Better. Thank you. You don't have to sleep in your clothes."

Luna chuckled. "It'll be okay. I'll just slide my jeans off." She sat up on the side of the bed and slipped the jeans down her body.

"Have you forgotten already that we have shared a bed before?" Marley teased as Luna slipped under the covers. "That's got to feel better."

"Yeah, it does. I was getting a crick in my neck."

"Snuggle in then."

Luna was thankful the only light in the room came from the bathroom. She was certain her face was flushed as she climbed into the warm bed next to Marley who had turned away from her. She stretched out on her back, her body barely touching Marley. She could feel the quiver of excitement creeping in and then soaring when Marley spoke.

"I said snuggle silly. Unless you're scared, I might hurl on you," Marley chuckled.

"No, I think you're past that stage." Luna turned on her side and moved close to Marley, carefully draping her arm across her waist. *Lord, please don't let her feel me trembling. Marley wouldn't understand how much she turns me on.*

"Doesn't that feel better?"

"Yes, it does. You're warm. Do you think you're running a fever?"

"I don't think so, just toasty warm under these covers." Marley grabbed Luna's hand and pulled her close. "Relax, I'm okay."

Luna felt her body soften as she melted into Marley's back. She could feel the warmth seeping through the thin fabric of Marley's shirt as she closed her eyes and willed sleep to take her.

†

An hour later, soft moans from Marley woke Luna. She was curled around Marley's body, her hand clasped with Marley's. She realized Marley was dreaming and she smiled wondering if Marley was having as beautiful a dream as she had been having before she woke. In her version of the dream, she and Marley were tangled in bedsheets, their bodies soaked with sweat from heated lovemaking. The content expression on Marley's face, made her relax and snuggle back into Marley and drift back to sleep.

CHAPTER NINE

When Marley woke hours later, she found she had turned and was entwined in Luna's arms. Luna looked so peaceful as she slept, a slight curve to her lips suggested a smile as her eyes moved side to side as she dreamed. *I wonder what she's dreaming about.* A lock of dark hair had fallen into Luna's face and she was tempted to brush it back, but she was afraid to move in fear of waking her sleeping friend. She had seen a much different side to Luna last night, from the playful womanizer she was accustomed to seeing. Luna had shown great compassion in caring for her at her most vulnerable when she was heaving her insides out. She was close enough that every time Luna let out a soft purring sound a warm breath caressed her skin. Marley wondered if Luna had ever fallen asleep in someone's arms or if she had strictly been a love them and leave them happy type of woman. She knew Luna had a reputation as a fantastic lover, but she'd never heard of her getting emotionally attached to anyone. In the years she had known her, she'd never known her to go home with the same woman more than once. What was it that made Luna tick? She was pondering that thought when Luna's eyes flew open and she pulled away from Marley.

"Oh, hey. I didn't realize where I was for a few seconds. Did I wake you with my snoring?"

"No, I think it was the growling of my stomach." Marley glanced at the clock. "I can't believe we slept so long. It's after eight."

"Wow. I guess we needed the rest. I've got to admit that was a great night of sleep for me."

"After you got into the bed?" Marley couldn't resist teasing Luna.

"Yeah, this bed's much more comfortable than your bench." Luna smiled and propped up on her elbow. "So, you're ready for an omelet?"

"I feel like I could eat a whole one by myself this morning, but I better stick to a half."

"Let me freshen up a bit and I'll start cooking. Do you want to shower?"

"That's probably a good idea. I woke up once soaked in sweat from breaking a fever." Marley groaned as she ran her hand through her hair. "Yes, definitely. I need to tame this bed head."

"If my opinion matters at all, I think you look adorable first thing in the morning." Luna slipped into her jeans and walked around the end of the bed.

"It matters a lot, thanks," Marley felt the heat rise to her face and turned away from Luna.

Luna headed toward the bathroom to wash her face. "Enjoy your shower then. Do you think your stomach can handle some coffee or apple juice?"

"Juice yes, but I don't think I can handle the acid in coffee just yet. Maybe, after I eat."

†

After Luna freshened up, she gave the bathroom over to Marley and walked into the kitchen to survey supplies. She opened the refrigerator and placed a bottle of apple juice into the freezer to get it chilled then removed ingredients for her monster omelet. She heard the water come on in the bathroom and began whipping up a half-dozen eggs in a bowl. She was busy cooking and didn't realize Marley had walked into the kitchen.

†

Marley propped against the door frame and watched Luna creating her masterpiece. Intensity was written all over her face as she carefully folded the egg concoction in the frying pan. She had seen that same intensity as she watched Luna working out. She was physical perfection in movement as she worked her body and Luna was no less intense in the kitchen. It was only when she spoke that Luna realized she had entered the kitchen. "That looks delicious."

Luna looked up to see Marley step into the kitchen. "Hey, welcome back. How do you feel?"

"Much better thank you. My stomach is growling to get a taste of that omelet. Is there anything I can help with?"

The toaster popped up. "Yes, you can get our toast, and pour some juice. I put it in the freezer to get it nice and cold."

125

"Perfect." Marley went to work pouring the juice.

"After we finish setting up the equipment, do you think you're up to walking through a workout? I don't want you lifting, but we can set up your routine."

"Yes, that would be nice. I'll work on some paperwork while y'all finish."

Luna cut the omelet in half and served it onto plates. Marley was seated at the table as she approached.

"You've got my mouth watering." Marley's eyes sparkled with excitement as Luna placed the plate in front of her.

"I say we forego hot sauce today." She chuckled as she took her seat.

"Yeah, I agree that probably wouldn't be a good idea."

Luna watched Marley as she took a bite. She moaned loudly.

"I didn't think this could taste better than the first, but this is heavenly." Marley took a long drink of the juice. "Damn, I feel like a sponge."

"You probably dehydrated a bit last night. Go slow though. Try not to gulp even though that's what your body is telling you to do."

Marley nodded as she took another bite. When there was only a small section left, Marley pushed her plate away. "I can't eat anymore."

"Do you mind if I finish for you?"

"Please do. It was too good to waste. I'll clean up if you want to take a shower before Pepper and Haley arrive."

"I can do both."

"No way. You've taken such good care of me, it's the least I can do, especially after such a nice breakfast. Go, and I'll see you later."

"It'll probably take us a couple of hours to get the last of the equipment set up and tested. Do you want me to come to get you when we're done?"

"Yeah, if I haven't already joined you."

"See you later." Luna smiled and left Marley's flat for her assigned one. She was thrilled to have her own private haven for the upstairs services, even though she would not be living on site. It gave her a space to freshen up and relax in private whenever she needed a break.

Luna keyed up her sound system and stripped out of her clothes. "Shower water to one twelve," she commanded as she entered her bathroom.

†

Marley stopped by her massage room to pick up some blank discs with the intention of downloading new music for massages while she organized her paperwork. Pepper and Haley were coming through the door as she left the room. "Good morning, you two."

"Hey, Boss. How are you doing?"

"Good, Pepper. Thanks. Luna will be down in a bit. She's taking a shower."

Pepper chuckled. "Did y'all have a good night out on the town?"

"We did until we had to cut the night short. I ended up getting sick on the way home."

Pepper frowned. "You okay?"

"I feel much better this morning. I think it was something I ate, or maybe a twenty-four-hour bug. A good night of sleep and a hot breakfast worked wonders."

Haley smiled at Marley, "It was probably a good thing Luna stayed out here last night then."

127

"She took very good care of me. I'd probably still be in bed in agony if she hadn't been there to tend to me last night."

"You need help with anything this morning?"

"Thanks, Haley, but I'm just going to do some paperwork and burn some new music."

"You can start the laundry and help us set up the equipment," Pepper said and placed an arm around her girlfriend's shoulders. "We'll see you later then."

†

Marley immersed herself in the music while she filed her paperwork and reviewed the final plans for the grand opening. All of the evaluations had been completed and the staff was excited about the new opportunities available to them. When she checked her watch, she found that three hours had passed since she entered the office. She removed the final cd from her computer and left the office. After dropping the music at her massage room, she continued down the hall to find Luna working out. She stopped to watch her movements. Every lift of her arms pulled her t-shirt up her torso and solid abs were evident. A light sheen of sweat glistened on her arms and legs and when she turned, Marley could see the back of her shirt soaked through. She took a deep breath and stepped into the room. "Sorry, I lost track of time."

Luna turned toward her and smiled. "No problem. I was just testing out some of the equipment. I went ahead and plotted out a routine for you. I hope you don't mind."

"Not at all. This is your specialty, so I trust you'll know what's best."

"Come with me then and we'll perform a walk through."

Marley listened carefully to Luna's instructions and on several occasions, Luna placed her strong hands on her body to correct a grip or movement. Confident in her skills as an instructor, Luna smiled when Marley correctly followed a sequence without complaint and even though they weren't doing an entire routine, Marley had broken out in a sweat. "Okay, that's enough for now. I don't want you to over-do things until you're back to one hundred percent. We have an incredibly busy week ahead of us and you need to be rested."

Luna handed her a towel to wipe her face. "If you're feeling better tomorrow, would you join me for some sushi?"

Marley wiped her face. "I'd love to."

"Great, can I call you tomorrow afternoon and we'll make it an early night?"

"That sounds wonderful. Thanks again for everything."

Luna smiled warmly at her. "You'd do the same for me."

"Yes, I would. But I still appreciate you caring for me."

"It was my pleasure." They started walking toward the stairs. "I'm going to grab my bag and head home. Call me if you need me."

"I'm going to take it easy and call it an early night. I promise, nothing strenuous."

"I'll see you tomorrow then." Luna disappeared upstairs as Marley walked back to her office to store her workout sheet and shut down her system. She heard Luna's bike growl as she walked back through the front room and decided to slip into the Roman bath to relax. She undressed and rinsed off in the shower before slipping into the hot water to soak her body. The warmth surrounded her and caressed her skin with a softness that reminded her of Luna's touch as she modified her grip or straightened her back as she performed her routine. She laid her head against the wall of the bath and closed her eyes. *Why am I thinking of Luna so much? Am I falling in love? Why do I crave the feel of her hands on my skin?* So many questions, with no answers in sight. Marley had always managed to ward off Luna's flirtations, knowing that her reputation as a player would only leave her broken-hearted, but lately, she had witnessed a change in Luna. Yes, she was one of the most popular requested staff by the members of the club, but Marley had come to grips with that. She too was now someone that gave pleasure to more than one woman, with no love or affection attached. It was a job, one that they were both excellent in performing, so in that sense, they were no different. Luna had been so busy with the start-up of the TWC that she didn't have the time or energy to hit the clubs for the one night stands she was famous for, but if given the time would she fall back into the routine? Was she willing to give the obvious connection they had a chance and risk having her heart broken? "So much to risk, but so much to gain."

The warm water soothed her body and within minutes, she felt relaxed and decided she would shower upstairs, grab a bite to eat and then crawl between the covers of her bed. She slipped into a robe and climbed the stairs to her flat. She showered and dressed for bed before stepping into the kitchen. She was surprised to find a note from Luna.

Thanks for a great morning. I hope you feel fantastic tonight!
Luna

She smiled and re-read the simple note several times as she made a sandwich and took a bottle of water from the refrigerator. She ate at her small table and felt her cheeks ache from smiling at the note. Maybe things are changing between us.

When she slipped between the sheets, she hugged the pillow Luna had slept on close to her body and buried her face in the scent lingering in the linens. She drifted off to sleep still smiling and dreamed of Luna.

†

The next few weeks flew by. The grand opening was even more successful than Lindy had anticipated and went off without a hitch. They were also so busy working with clients that Marley had seen very little of Luna, and she found that she missed the intimate time they had shared prior to opening full time. Even Lindy had been pulled away to deal with professional obligations. Marley had her booked for a Friday night massage and was waiting in her office for her to arrive. Luna popped her head into the room. "I've got a couple of appointments tonight, but would you like to grab something to eat later?"

"That sounds great. We haven't seen much of each other for a couple of weeks."

"So, you miss seeing me, like I miss you?"

Marley couldn't resist the grin on Luna's face. "Yes, I do. It's been crazy busy."

"I should be done by seven. What about you?"

"It depends on what's going on with Lindy. I have her session coming up, but I'm not sure if she wants more."

"If she is me, I most certainly do, if you're up to it," Lindy said as she stopped beside Luna.

"Hey, Boss," Luna said.

"Good evening ladies. Sorry for eavesdropping, but I'd love an appointment with Marley after my massage."

"No problem. I'll see you later." Luna left to prepare for her appointments.

Marley smiled up at Lindy. "I have the room ready when you are."

"Let me slip out of these clothes into a robe and I'll be right there."

"I'll be waiting." Marley followed her from the office and went to the massage room. She checked the warming oil and turned on some of the new music and waited for Lindy.

Lindy stepped inside. "I am so ready for your magic hands."

"Rough week?"

"It's been more busy than usual, but it's over and now I can get some relaxation with you. How has business been here?"

"It couldn't be better. The members seem to be very happy and the staff is really enjoying working here. Lay down and I'll have you relaxed in no time."

"I do love the sound of that." Lindy laid down on her stomach and Marley started her massage.

"You are tense. Let me know if I go too deep."

Lindy chuckled. "That sounded so sexual coming from you."

Without thinking, Marley smacked Lindy's ass. "You know what I meant, silly."

"Oh, that felt good." Lindy's voice dropped to a purr.

"Sorry, that was just a reflex."

"I didn't mind at all."

Marley shook her head at her behavior as she continued the massage. It may have been an unprofessional action, but she felt Lindy's muscles begin to relax as she kneaded deeply into her muscles.

"Is this new music?"

"Yes, it is. Do you like it?"

"Very much so. It's got a sensual sound and its effect, with the rhythm of your hands, is incredibly relaxing."

"It's from the tantric genre, inspired for sensuality and arousal."

"It's definitely working."

Marley smiled and continued working down Lindy's body. When she finished and asked her to roll over, she could see the puckering of Lindy's nipples, exposing her arousal. She added more of the warm oil and began massaging the base of her neck. "Do you have big plans for the weekend?"

"I plan to come for a workout tomorrow and maybe hit the sauna and bath. Sunday, I'm sleeping in as long as possible. What about you?"

"We have a light schedule tomorrow, so a bit of relaxing here too. Luna and I have been talking about maybe looking at some new cars, so we may do some window shopping."

"That's always fun. What are you looking for?"

"I think Luna wants a Jeep and I've always dreamed of a Land Rover."

"If you find something you like, work with Danna. I'm sure she can arrange good deals for you both."

"I will definitely keep that in mind. We can always use a good deal."

"She thinks very highly of both of you, so I'm sure she'll make it work. It's good to have connections."

"Yes, I'm learning that quickly."

"Are you still happy here Marley?"

"Very much so. This is a dream come true for many of us."

"For the members as well. The ladies have gushed about the staff and the services provided. I think even a few of them enjoy coming for workouts now." Marley chuckled at her comment. "What better way to relive tired, stiff muscles, and the bedroom boredom at home?"

"The way I see it, it's a win-win situation all around."

"As long as our libidos don't wear you ladies out. I worry you don't have much time for your own social life being so committed to the success of the club."

"I think the extra activity may slow down a bit once the members realize it's not a passing thing and we will be here to provide services. I think they are enjoying the experimenting of the variety of techniques offered and will settle into their favorites eventually."

"Well, I certainly have mine. You and Luna provide everything I could ask for."

Marley felt her cheeks flushing. "Thank you."

"Speaking of Luna. You seem to be drawing closer. Have you given any further consideration to the two of you evolving to more than friends?"

"We have become closer over these past few weeks, but that's all." Marley felt the heat rushing through her body. She knew she was lying. She was falling in love with Luna and nothing could stop the train wreck of emotions that were going through her mind every time she thought of Luna.

"I just hope you won't sacrifice your need for companionship to ensure the members' desires. Your long-term leadership here is very important to our success."

Marley chuckled. "I'll take that under advisement, Boss."

"Not just as your employer, but as a friend as well."

"I do consider you to be a friend. You've given me so much already, but I promise I won't let life pass me by without finding hope for love."

"Now we're talking. I do love the L word."

"How are things going with Jay Dub?"

"Same old same old. He's so busy with this case and who knows what else, I haven't seen much of him. I'm usually satisfied and asleep before he comes home. I'm pretty certain he is satisfied too."

Marley could feel the tension creeping back into Lindy's body and mentally kicked herself for bringing up the sensitive subject. She focused her skillful hands on the insides of Lindy's thighs to bring her back to a state of relaxed arousal.

"Damn, you know how to make a woman feel great. I hope you didn't mind an impromptu session tonight."

"I'd never turn you down. You should know you're my number one," Marley replied and winked at Lindy.

"I bet you say that to all the women."

"Absolutely not. I've kept my clientele down to a minimum. The others don't mind the extra attention and it gives me time to focus on management."

Marley's thumb stroked softly across Lindy's swollen clit. "I do love you focusing on management," she replied after gasping from Marley's touch. "I'm ready to go upstairs to work on those management skills with you."

"Run through a shower while I clean up the room and I'll meet you in just a few minutes."

Marley offered her hand to Lindy to help her off the massage table. "Steady on those legs now," she teased. "Anything special you'd care for tonight?"

"I want you and your strap on deep inside me tonight," Lindy admitted. "I need a good hard fucking."

"As you wish. I'll get the room ready."

She watched Lindy leave the room and began cleaning and reorganizing the massage room, before rushing upstairs to her business flat to prepare for Lindy's arrival. The sheets were pulled back and extra pillows placed when Lindy arrived in a robe. Her freshly showered body was already flushed with arousal as Marley slipped the robe off Lindy's shoulder with a tender kiss. Lindy relaxed onto the bed. "I'll be back in just a moment." She turned on music that would start off slow and build to a pulsing beat which would provide an excellent rhythm for fucking, then slipped into the bathroom. She stripped out of her uniform and fastened a harness around her hips. Luna had purchased a few new toys for her and she placed one of them on the mount, securing it in a position that would provide them both maximum pleasure. She donned a robe and returned to the bedroom and turned the lights down low. She removed the robe and Lindy's eyes fell below her waist, her eyes hungrily appreciating the size and length of the new toy.

"I look forward to feeling that inside me," she growled with anticipation.

"A new purchase I thought you might enjoy." She entered the bed and lay next to Lindy, the toy grazing the skin on her thigh as Marley moved closer. The music was still soft as her hand and mouth began exploring Lindy's body. She could feel the arousal growing for Lindy as her body arched to meet her every touch and the scent of excitement filled the bed. Lindy's tongue danced wildly in her mouth and she groaned deeply when Marley's hand cupped her vagina. She could feel the wetness and heat filling her hand as she gave it a soft squeeze.

"Oh, hell yes," Lindy cried when Marley slipped a finger inside to test her readiness. "I need you deep inside me."

Marley reached over for a tube of lubricant and poured it into Lindy's eager hand. She could feel the tug of the straps pressed against her clit as Lindy's hand slid up and down the shaft of the dildo, covering it with the silky lube. When Lindy had finished coating, Marley grabbed a pillow and positioned it beneath Lindy's hips raising her off the bed. She maneuvered her body between Lindy's legs and placed the tip of the shaft in Lindy's opening. Marley looked into Lindy's passion filled eyes as she leaned forward, lowered her hips, slowly sinking the dildo into her body. The music began with a slow pulse and Marley easily matched the rhythm, which grew perfectly with Lindy's desire. Using a strap on used muscles Marley didn't often use, but she could feel the improvements she had gained in the few weeks of workouts Luna had designed for her. She could feel the power of her thrusts as her energy entered Lindy, eliciting loud groans of pleasure as she grabbed the sheets in an effort to build her climax to its highest peak. Marley lost herself in the music, allowing the beat to become one with her body as she gave pleasure to Lindy. She finally understood Luna's description of losing control to the music and the sound of her lover as she thrust deeply inside them. Just the thought of Luna made it difficult for Marley to hold back the orgasm from the straps rubbing across her clit with each movement of her hips. She was relieved when Lindy called out and her body began convulsing, her arm covering her mouth to prevent a scream. With a final deep thrust, Marley came with a similar result, her body quaking from the exertion of making love to Lindy and she barely caught her body from collapsing on top of her. She rested her weight on her elbows, the dildo buried inside Lindy. A bead of sweat dripped from her chin onto Lindy's chest as they struggled to gain their breath.

Lindy looked into her eyes, "Holy shit, where have you been hiding that girl?"

"I'm not exactly sure where that came from. I didn't hurt you, did I?"

"Heavens no, that was fucking fantastic. Excuse the pun."

"For a moment I just got lost in the music." She moved to begin removing the dildo from Lindy's body, but Lindy stopped her.

"Not yet, unless you're uncomfortable."

Marley stopped her movements and relaxed on her elbows. She noticed Lindy grinning at her. "You want more don't you?"

"That was so good. Do you have another one in you?"

"I think so."

"Let's try a position that will be easier for you."

"Tell me what you want, and I'll make it happen."

"Stand up beside the bed and I'll get up on my knees. I want you to take me from behind with that monster of yours. I can help with the motion to make it easier for you."

"Did you have this planned all along?"

"I had no idea you would be so proficient, and I'd love another orgasm like that. You okay with that?"

"Absolutely. I missed my workout today." Marley chuckled. "Or so I thought I did. That did feel fantastic though."

"Do you need a break before we go again?"

"I could use a bit of water?"

"I'll get us both a bottle. Are you ready?"

Lindy nodded and Marley slowly withdrew the dildo from her body and rolled off the bed. The toy dangled between her thighs as she walked to the kitchen for the water. When she returned to the bed, Lindy was sitting up on the side watching her.

"That is a very alluring sight on you."

"To be honest, I feel a little silly."

"There is nothing silly about the way you handled that." She motioned toward the dildo with the opened bottle of water she'd accepted from Marley. "That was some serious fucking."

Marley smiled. "Glad you approve, Ma'am." She tapped her bottle against Lindy's. "Drink up." She took a long drink from her bottle, capped it and reached back for Lindy's. She saw the lubricant on the table. "Do you need more lube?"

"Ha! You must be kidding. I'll add some for you though." She reached out her hand.

Marley poured more lube into her hand and stepped forward. She watched Lindy's hand slide up and down the shaft, marveling at the sensual movement she used to spread the lube.

"There, that should be good." Lindy turned around on the bed and raised up to her knees. "This looks like a good height for you."

Marley moved closer to the edge of the bed to find Lindy's hips just lower than her own. "This will do just fine." She lifted the dildo between Lindy's legs. "Would you care to do the honors?" she teased as she rubbed the toy against Lindy's lips.

Lindy took the head of the toy and inserted the tip inside her opening. "All set."

Marley leaned forward and felt the dildo sink deep into Lindy.

"Oh yeah baby, that feels good. Fuck me hard, Marley."

The mood of the music shifted again and Marley closed her eyes and took Lindy's hips in her hands and began rocking into her body, her hips slapping against Lindy's ass with each forward thrust. She felt Lindy pushing back against her, adding to the depth of her strokes. The resistance of the dildo against the harness straps sent delicious waves of pleasure through Marley as she plunged faster and deeper into Lindy. She felt a bead of sweat trickle down the center of her back and lifted her right foot onto the bed adding a bit of an angle to her thrusts, reaching a highly erogenous spot inside Lindy causing her to call out in pleasure.

"Yes, yes, that's it, Marley. Oh, fuck yes."

Marley was amazed her body could keep up with the frantic pulse of the music, but she found herself moving without thought as she fucked Lindy wildly, until she cried out and flew forward on the bed. Gasping for breath, Marley slipped down to her knees beside the bed, breathless with sweat pouring down her legs.

Several minutes later, Lindy managed to roll onto her back and sit up. She took Marley's face in her hands and kissed her deeply. When she broke the kiss, she reached to help Marley stand. "Remove the harness and come snuggle with me for a few minutes. I have something I want to ask you."

Intrigued, Marley stood and walked to the bathroom. She took the harness off and placed it in the sink. She grabbed a hand towel and wiped her face and looked at her image in the mirror. *Holy shit. I can't believe I just did that. Twice even and enjoyed it too.* She grinned and dropped the towel on the counter. She returned to the bedroom and took a long drink of water. "Are you thirsty?"

"I already drained the bottle. I'm good."

Marley stretched out on the bed and Lindy rolled onto her side and propped her head on her elbow. "Why do you look like the cat that ate the canary?"

"Because I have something that I'd like to ask you, but I don't know how to approach the topic."

"I think we've always been honest, so just ask. What is it you want?"

Marley watched as Lindy licked her lips as she struggled to find the right words. "I've never experienced a threesome before and I'd like to."

Marley's eyes widened, but she refrained from responding for several seconds while her heart was stuck in her throat. "Um, I've never done that either."

"Really, so it would be a first for you too? I mean if you're interested."

"Yes, it would. What did you have in mind?"

"I would like to be with you and Luna at the same time."

"Luna! Lindy, I don't know about that. You know how I feel about her."

"I know how you claim you used to feel about her, but I sense that's changed."

"Oh Lindy, I don't know about this." Marley shifted on the bed, suddenly uncomfortable.

Lindy reached up to stroke Marley's face. "I don't expect an answer right now. I just want you to consider my request. I will be disappointed if you decline, but I will honor your decision and never repeat the request if it's not comfortable for either of you."

"Have you mentioned this to Luna?"

"No, I wanted to approach you first. I have a feeling that Luna would jump at any chance to be with you."

"You really think so?"

"I'd bet my life on it. That woman adores you."

"Do you plan to mention it to her?"

It was Lindy's turn to shift uncomfortably. "I was kinda hoping you would broach the subject if you decide you are interested."

"Really?"

"Of course, I would make it well worth it to both of you for your time, but the experience would mean so much more to me than money."

Marley scanned Lindy's face and knew her request was genuine and pleading. That was something she'd never seen in Lindy's eyes before. "I'll find a way to bring it up to Luna."

"Thanks for not giving me an outright 'no.'"

"But it's not a 'yes' yet, either. I've got a bunch of thinking to do."

Lindy leaned forward and kissed her excitedly. "That's enough to keep me hoping." She scooted down to the end of the bed. "I've got to get moving. I'll see you tomorrow, okay?"

"Yes, sure. Have a great night."

"I left you an envelope on your desk. See ya!"

†

Lindy left the flat and Marley laid back on the pillows. "Now what have I gotten myself into?" She was tempted to pull the covers up and fall asleep until she remembered she and Luna were going to dinner. If she got her butt in gear, she could strip the bed, put away her harness and toys and still have some time in the sauna before she would need to shower and dress for dinner. She stripped the bed and placed the soiled linens in a pillowcase she'd set outside the flat. She'd replace the linens and take the soiled ones to launder. Marley wrapped her body in the thick robe and went to work. She cleaned the dildo and placed it with the harness in a drawer in the bedroom. She picked up the linens to carry them downstairs. She smiled at the sounds of pleasure as she passed by Luna's flat and descended the stairs. Haley looked up as she arrived at the front desk. "I'm going to be in the sauna if you need anything."

"Enjoy." Haley took the linens and walked toward the laundry.

Marley was relieved when no one was using the sauna. She didn't mind company, but she had so much to consider regarding Lindy's proposal. She was looking for some sweat and a quiet place to help her think things through. She climbed onto the second level and stretched out, ignoring the front of her robe falling open. Right now, she just didn't care. There were very few people left in the club and with few exceptions they had seen her naked before. She felt the heat wrap around her body and her pores opened to purge her body of the toxins and excess fluid built up in her tissues. Marley closed her eyes and drifted until the buzzer sounded thirty minutes later to notify her the cycle had ended. She pushed up to a seated decision. She hadn't found the answers she was hoping to find, but her body felt better. Marley left the sauna and took the back entrance to her flat, keying in the code to open her door.

The cool air hit her with a blast as soon as the door opened, and she spoke to increase the temperature as she walked to the refrigerator for a bottle of water. She walked to her closet to decide on an outfit while her body temperature returned to normal. She settled on jeans and a black, long-sleeved polo, then dug out a well-worn pair of loafers. She finished her water, dressed and spritzed on a bit of scent. As she opened the door to exit her flat, Luna was about to knock. Her hand was raised, and the look of surprise filled her face when the door opened. Marley's eyes traveled down Luna's body. A black form-fitting shirt was tucked inside black jeans, topped off by black boots. "Damn, is there anything you don't look great in?"

Luna shrugged. "Maybe a dress or bikini."

"Maybe the dress, but I bet you'd rock a bikini."

"I'm more board shorts and body glove shirt type." She smiled. "You're looking great yourself."

"Thanks."

"Have you worked up an appetite?"

Marley smiled, her mind wandering back to her session with Lindy. "I could eat. Where are we heading tonight?"

"I could use some carbs. You up for Italian?"

"Come on, I'll drive."

†

Hours later, after gorging themselves on pasta, salad and bread dipped in a seasoned oil mixture, Luna pushed back her plate. "I was hungry, but I can never finish portions this size."

"No worries, they'll taste even better tomorrow."

"Are you feeling okay?"

Marley cocked her head to the side. "Yes, why?"

"You seem preoccupied tonight."

"Sorry, it's been a long few weeks."

"Yes, it has. We only have a few appointments tomorrow, so we'll close early. We can handle things if you want to take the day off."

Marley was finding it difficult to keep her eyes off Luna and her thoughts drifted back to Lindy's request. She had never expected to see this side of Luna. She had been getting glimpses of, someone who was genuine in caring for others. Maybe she had judged her too harshly. Luna and she had developed a closer friendship in their new roles, and she was quick to give her a smile that made her feel special. Something was very different between them lately.

"I just need a good night's sleep. I'd like to get a work out in tomorrow and maybe some bath time."

"That does sound good. Would you mind some company in the bath?"

"I was hoping you'd join me."

When the waiter returned with their leftovers in a bag, Luna paid the bill. Marley attempted to pay, but she was quickly reminded that Luna had asked her to dinner. "Do you want to still do some car gazing this weekend?"

Marley smiled up at Luna. "Let's plan on Sunday afternoon when there won't be salesmen there to harass us. Lindy said to pick out what we like and let Danna work out deals for us."

"Funny you should mention Danna. She said basically the same thing. Pick out what we like, and she'll make sure we're treated well."

"Are you ready to buy?"

"I've got ample funds for a very nice down payment. With my salary, I won't have any problem making a payment and getting it paid off quickly."

"Let's do this then," Marley answered as she stood and walked to Luna's side.

"I've never had a new vehicle," Luna said. "Always used or hand me downs from my dad."

"I had one and she's served me well for years, but it's time she goes to someone new."

They returned to the club and Luna handed Marley the bag. "Why don't you keep these for lunch tomorrow?"

"I can do that. Are you headed home now?"

"I think we could both do with a good night's sleep. I'll see you in the morning."

"For breakfast? I can cook this time," she offered.

Luna turned back toward her and Marley could see her smile in the dim lighting. "Breakfast sounds great. See you at nine?"

"That will be perfect. Ride safe."

"Always."

Marley watched Luna straddle the bike and then drive away, before entering the club and setting the security code. She climbed the stairs to her flat and placed the leftovers in the refrigerator. After changing into a t-shirt and sweats,

Marley stretched out on her couch and turned the television on to find a Southeastern Conference football game in progress. As hard as she tried to get into the game, Marley's thoughts kept wandering back to her conversation with Lindy and her bold request. *Am I ready to take the next step with Luna? I think Lindy is correct. We seem destined to be together. So why am I hesitating? Am I afraid my heart will be broken and it will ruin our working relationship? Is it really any different than sleeping with the members? Heck yeah, I don't have feelings for any of them. Wait, did I really admit that to myself? Am I falling in love with Luna? Yes, I think I am.*

Marley left the couch and removed her sweat pants before climbing into bed. She found she was more drained than she thought and slipped quickly off to sleep. Her dreams were filled with Luna and what it would be like their first time together. When she woke, the dreams lingered and she realized she wanted something for herself. She needed to be intimate with Luna before they agreed to be with Lindy. Selfishly, she didn't want to share that experience with anyone else. She glanced at the clock and shot up straight in the bed. "Oh shit, I agreed to cook breakfast."

She took a quick shower and dressed in shorts and a t-shirt before going to the kitchen. There was no way she could top Luna's omelets, so she settled on bacon and French toast. She started the bacon cooking while she brewed a cup of coffee. She placed a container of syrup in a pot of water to warm it and pulled out the butter and eggs. She whipped up the egg concoction and added a bit of cinnamon to the mixture of egg and milk. She placed the juice in the freezer and set two place settings at the table. She knew Luna was punctual, so she started cooking the French toast just before nine to keep it hot for Luna's arrival. She had just taken the first two slices out and covered them with butter when Luna knocked on her door. "Come on in," she called out.

"I smell bacon, bacon, bacon! I haven't had that in ages."

"Yes, you do, and I'm hoping you like French Toast."

"Like it, no, I love it. Is there anything I can do?"

"You can pour some juice and carry the bacon to the table. I'll have two more slices done in a minute if you want to bring your plate." Marley screwed up her face in thought. "I forgot about you being such a healthy eater. I should have chosen something better."

"Nonsense, I need to treat myself from time to time and this is perfect. No worries. I'll have this worked off in no time."

"I wish I had your metabolism," Marley chuckled as she walked toward the table.

"This is fantastic," Luna praised when they sat down to eat.

"Glad you like it." They both easily devoured two slices. "Can you do one more?"

"At least one," Luna grinned.

"Sit tight then." Marley cooked two more slices for Luna and another for herself." She finished eating before Luna and when she looked over at her, Luna had a drop of syrup on the corner of her mouth threatening to run down her chin. Luna was so intent on eating she didn't realize the syrup was there. Without a second thought, Marley leaned over to Luna and licked the syrup from her mouth with the tip of her tongue.

Luna's eyes grew wide from Marley's gesture. She looked over at Marley, who was smiling at her.

"Sorry, I couldn't resist."

"No need to apologize, but hand me that syrup will ya so I can coat my face."

Marley broke out laughing.

"This really was a great breakfast."

"I'm glad you enjoyed it. No way was I going to try to imitate your omelettes."

"They aren't hard to make. I can teach you if you'd like."

"I'd like that. What time is Lindy scheduled this morning?"

"Ten thirty. Do you want to work out with us?"

"Would you mind?"

"Absolutely not. I'm sure Lindy wouldn't mind seeing me torturing someone else too."

"Maybe I should reconsider then."

"Nope, too late to back out now."

"Is she the only appointment today?"

"No. Pepper has someone coming in also, and I think there's a massage scheduled too. After that, the club is all ours. I'm looking forward to soaking in the bath."

"Me too." Marley finished her juice and rinsed the dishes to place them in the dishwasher.

†

Luna returned the syrup and butter to the refrigerator and was taking her juice glass to Marley when she turned around and they were mere inches apart. Without a second thought, she reached for Marley and leaned in for a kiss. Gentle at first, she was surprised when Marley's lips parted, inviting her tongue inside for a slow, sensual kiss. Marley's hands cupped Luna's face and when the kiss ended, she smiled at Luna.

"Wow."

"Yeah, wow. That felt wonderful."

"We have things to talk about later," Marley said.

148

Luna looked confused. "Good things, or something else?"

"I think it will all be good."

"Can we do it now?"

"No, we need to finish work today, then we'll have all afternoon to talk."

Luna's face turned into a frown. "You've got me worried."

Marley initiated the second kiss, and when she broke it, she whispered. "Don't worry. Just trust me on this."

†

Luna nodded and left the flat, her head whirling, and her thoughts spinning off in a thousand directions. I don't think there's anything I've done wrong, so I can't be in trouble. Besides Marley said everything was good, so I'll have to trust her. Damn, that was cruel of her to mention something and then make her worry for hours. I'll have to figure out a way to pay her back for that. She grinned to herself and took the stairs eager to start the day.

Lindy was coming in the front door as Luna hit the bottom of the stairs. "Good morning, Boss. Are you ready for a workout?"

"I will be in just a few minutes. I need to drop my bag and I'll meet you in the gym."

"Would you mind if Marley joined us for a workout this morning?"

Lindy smiled at the offer. "No, not at all. It will give me someone to commiserate with as you work us to death. I've only got an hour to work out today though. I've got an engagement I need to attend today."

"That's no problem. We'll finish up in plenty of time for you to shower and be on your way. I'll see you in a few then." Luna grabbed fresh towels and walked to the workout room.

†

Lindy dropped her bag and hung her outfit in the locker room and then swung by the office to see if Marley was there. She was surprised to find the envelope she had left for her still sitting on the desk. *I hope I didn't jeopardize my relationship with Marley with my request. She's working out with us this morning, so it can't be that. Maybe she's just been too busy to collect her fee.*

When she walked into the gym, Marley had already arrived and was talking with Luna. She could feel the electricity in the air between them and smiled as they turned in her direction. *There is definitely something growing here.* "I hear you are to be my partner in torture this morning Marley."

"Oh, come on, it's never that bad," Luna remarked.

"Easy for you to say. You've got the body of a goddess," Lindy replied.

"Made from hard work, so let's get busy ladies and start stretching. Lindy's on a timeline this morning."

It didn't take long for Luna to have them both sweating as she put them through their routines. She would walk between Lindy and Marley, correcting posture during an exercise, using her hands and instructions to show them the correct methods. Neither of them complained of the personal touch as Luna was always gentle in her approach. She kept an eye on the clock and when it was near the time to halt the exercise, Luna called them together to sit on the floor. "That was quite a workout for both of you this morning. I want you to end it with some gentle stretching to relax and help your muscles cool down."

150

Lindy admired the way the uniform fit Luna's body as she moved along with them. The choice of the bright colors accented her dark skin, and her muscles seemed to ripple below the fabric. *Down girl, she spoke to her inner child. Now is definitely not the time to play.* She found herself grinning and invigorated by the workout and bounced up from the floor. "Thanks for a great workout and great company, Ladies. I'll see you both on Monday."

"Have a great rest of your weekend, Boss," Luna said as she and Marley also stood.

"Enjoy your car shopping tomorrow," Lindy tossed back at them as she walked toward the door.

"We will," Marley called back to answer.

†

When she turned back to Luna, she found her smiling. "Are you ready for some time in the bath?"

"Let me just freshen up here and drop off the towels while you rinse off." Luna picked up the used towels and was in the process of cleaning the equipment when Marley left.

"I'll meet you in the bath."

†

Lindy had undressed and was about to step into the shower when Marley arrived. "I hope I didn't scare you off with my request yesterday."

"I wasn't expecting that conversation, I'll admit, but no, I'm not scared. I've been thinking about it a lot, and plan to broach the subject with Luna today."

151

"That sounds promising." Lindy grinned and stepped into the shower. "I'll keep everything I have crossed that it goes well."

"Thanks, Boss," Marley said as she removed her workout clothes and tossed them in a dirty clothes bag. She grabbed a fresh towel and walked into the shower to rinse the workout sweat from her body. She lingered in the shower, enjoying the feel of the water pulsing against her skin and when she turned the water off and reached for a towel, the locker room was silent. Lindy had already dressed and was gone. Marley patted her skin dry and slipped a thick robe over her body. She tossed the wet towel in the bin and made a stop by her office. She saw the envelope sitting on her desk. She had forgotten all about it after her conversation with Lindy. She opened it to find four one-hundred-dollar bills and slipped the envelope deep in the back drawer of her desk, where several other envelopes were stashed. Those will easily make a healthy down payment on a new car. She smiled and closed the drawer. Now to talk to Luna.

†

Luna had wiped down the equipment and took care of the dirty towels before walking into the Roman bath to rinse off in the shower and wait for Marley. She was already sitting in the bath, enjoying the water when Marley walked into the room. Her heart began to race as Marley took her robe off, hung it on a hook and walked naked toward the pool. *She is beautiful. Moves with such cat-like grace I feel myself watching her every move.*

"How's the water?" Marley asked as she carefully took the first step into the bath.

"Heavenly," she answered as she reached for Marley's hand. "Even better now that you're here."

"You are such a smooth talker," Marley teased. "Damn, this does feel good though."

Marley sat beside Luna and laid her head back against the headrest designed in the edge of the bath and closed her eyes. She moaned softly as the water caressed her skin.

"So, what's all this mysterious conversation about you alluded to this morning? That was pretty cruel of you by the way."

Marley popped an eye open and looked at Luna. "Can a girl get five minutes of peace and quiet?"

"Okay, five minutes, but you're driving me crazy."

Marley smiled. "I know. It's payback for giving me three extra minutes on the treadmill." She closed her eyes and smiled.

"Damn."

"Uh, uh, five minutes," Marley repeated.

Luna slumped back in her seat and stared at the painfully slow ticking clock. When the final seconds ticked away, she turned to Marley who was watching her. "Okay, spill it."

"Thank you for giving me five minutes."

"You're welcome. Please? The suspense is killing me."

"Okay, so yesterday I had my normal Friday massage appointment with Lindy, and then she wanted an extra session. She was in an unusual mood and asked for me to use a strap on with her."

"I take it that's not a norm with you? I use it often with her."

"No, not at all. A first actually. Which, started a conversation with her afterward."

"About?"

"Firsts, and never ever. Lindy is an incredible woman."

"I agree with that. I take it she kinda blew you away with something, with the way you've been acting the last twenty-four hours."

"She did indeed, and it's forced me to think about the future seriously."

Luna turned toward her quickly making the water between them splash into Marley's face. "You're not leaving the club, are you?"

Marley wiped the water out of her face. "No, nothing like that. I love it here. What she asked, involves you, and I had a lot of thinking to do about my past decisions to stay away from you because of your reputation as a player. Your one and done history, I'll admit was a huge factor in that decision."

"I have my own reasons for that, but I'll hear you out. What is it that Lindy wants that has you so conflicted?"

Marley felt herself taking a deep breath. She hadn't figured out a way to gently ease into the conversation, so she just blurted it out in one breath, "So, Lindy has never experienced a threesome."

"Really? That's kind of surprising. I thought everyone had done it at least once." Luna chuckled as she watched Marley's face.

"Hey, now. I haven't either," Marley informed her with a scowl. "Some of us, aren't as experienced as others when it comes to sex."

"Okay, I'll take that. So, what has you so nervous?"

"She wants her first experience to be with you and me?" Marley saw the recognition of Lindy's request bring a scowl to Luna's face. She was glad it was only temporary as Luna then smiled.

"Hence the dilemma?"

"Yes."

"What's your biggest concern?"

"Honestly, I don't want our first experience together to be with someone else. I'd prefer it to just be the two of us."

Luna's eyebrows raised. "Are you saying that you'd be interested in having sex with me? Finally?"

"No."

"No, you don't want to do this? Why are we having this conversation at all then?"

Marley watched Luna turn away from her to hide the hurt on her face. Marley reached out and took Luna's chin in her hand and turned her face to her. She could see the tears in Luna's eyes. "I don't want to have sex with you. I want to make love with you."

A tear slid down Luna's right cheek and Marley brushed it away. "Do I need to say it again?"

"Yes, please."

"I want to make love with you, Luna."

"You have no idea how long I've longed to hear those words. I want you to know that I've changed. I don't want anyone but you. I know we both give pleasure to the members of the club, but as you've mentioned, that's sex, not lovemaking."

"I've felt that change in you, and that played a large part in my decision."

"Have you agreed to Lindy's request?"

"No, but I told her that I'd discuss it with you."

"Is that something you really want to do?"

"She's done so much for both of us, but she assured me there was no pressure if we declined her offer. To be honest, I can't think of two women I'd rather have my first experience with."

"Wow, this is so not what I thought we'd be talking about today."

"What did you think?"

"I had no clue, so you've blown me out of the water."

"Do we tell her yes?"

"I think that depends on us. We may make love and realize it's not at all what we envisioned it to be."

"Do you really think that will happen?"

"No, but we may decide we don't want to share us, with anyone else."

Marley raised her hand to Luna's forehead, in a mock effort to check her temperature. "My you have changed. That was a romantic thing to admit."

Luna stuck her bottom lip out in a pout. "I can be very romantic."

"I'm certain you can be."

"When I'm inspired."

Marley grinned. "Now you know one of my never ever things, but I don't know yours."

Luna closed her eyes in thought. When she opened them again, she looked at Marley, "I've never had a professional massage."

"I can handle that today. With great pleasure. I've been dying to get my hands on that body of yours."

"You could have at any time. You know how much I adore you, right?"

"Yes, but the timing wasn't right. It is now."

Luna leaned into her and kissed Marley. Each kiss felt better than the last, and now she had hope that they would only continue to get better.

"Let's relax here for a bit and then we can heat up those leftovers. Afterward, if you're ready for a massage, we can take it from there."

†

After soaking for a short while, Marley opened her eyes to find Luna, with her head resting on the wall of the bath and her arms stretched along the wall. She quietly moved in front of Luna and straddled her outstretched legs. She lowered her body into Luna's lap and smiled when Luna's eyes popped open. Luna remained silent, watching every move Marley made as she stretched out her arms and used her fingertips to trace from the bed of her palms, down the length of her arms and up to frame her face. Marley felt Luna shiver in the heated bath and recognized the desire burning in Luna's eyes as she leaned her body forward and kissed her deeply. *Yes, this feels so right.* She continued the kiss until they were nearly breathless and then, rested her body back on Luna's legs.

"Wow, I hope that felt as good to you as it did for me," Marley whispered.

Luna raised her hand to stroke Marley's face. "I have a confession to make."

Marley cocked an eyebrow. "Oh really? Do tell."

Luna locked eyes with Marley. "When you kiss me like that, for a few seconds my whole world turns black, like nothing else matters but the feeling of your kiss."

"That's a relief. I thought it was just me. Nothing like that has ever happened before for me."

"Me either, but it's an amazing feeling. Like a small orgasm, all in itself."

"That is a perfect description for it." Marley smiled and leaned forward for another kiss. "Do you think this could be our sign that maybe it's time for us to be together?"

Luna's devilish grin returned. "I sure hope so. I want you so badly, more so than ever before."

"Soon, I think," Marley said, as she stood and offered Luna her hand.

CHAPTER TEN

After eating the leftovers, Marley and Luna sat at the table in their robes from the bath. "I do believe that was even better than last night."

Luna patted her stomach. "Without a doubt. That will always be one of my favorite places to eat."

"Mine too. Would you like more tea?"

"Yes, a bit if you don't mind. I never dreamed I'd enjoy sweet tea so much."

"It can be addicting. I should have warned you."

Luna smiled as she took the refilled glass from Marley. "You should have."

"I'm finding out there are many things about you are addicting." Luna reached out to pull Marley into her lap. Her eye's searched Marley's and saw a look of desire deep in them. "One of them being your kissable lips." She leaned into a kiss. "So sweet and intoxicating."

"I am so enjoying this romantic side of you, but don't let it replace the cocky side of you."

"What cocky side?"

"The one that's confident about everything she does and knows she's the best."

"That's not really me. I hope you know that. It's just a persona. I actually question myself if I'm ever enough."

"You are perfect, just as you are."

"All that matters, is that you think so." Luna wrapped her up in another kiss, and when it ended, Marley was nearly breathless.

"I think we'd better head downstairs if you're going to get a massage today. Give me a minute to change."

"Please don't."

"Please don't what?"

"Don't change. I want you to be nude as you massage me."

"That is highly unprofessional, Miss."

"It's just you and I, and I promise I won't tell anyone."

"Okay, Miss Cocky, let's go." Marley stood and pulled Luna to her feet. "It will take a few minutes to warm the oil."

"I know what we can do while we wait," Luna said as she puckered her lips.

"C'mon you," Marley reached for her hand and led her downstairs.

"Ooh, the inner sanctum."

"That's right. The gym is your domain, and this is mine. You can have a seat on the table while I get ready."

Luna slid back to take a seat as directed while Marley turned on the warmer and placed a bottle of oils inside.

†

Then she turned on soft music. Marley was tempted to use the same music she had used with Lindy, but had second thoughts. "Are there any tender areas or ticklish spots I should be aware of before we start?"

"My shoulder muscles have been tight lately, and my toes are ticklish."

She grinned. "I'll keep that in mind. Off with that robe, Ma'am. Do you want a sheet to cover you?"

"Only if you recommend one."

"No sheet then. Roll over onto your stomach please." Marley stepped back to allow Luna to position her body comfortably on the table. "How does that feel? The face padding okay?"

"Very comfortable."

"Good, just close your eyes and let the music sink into you."

Marley stood back and marveled at the beautiful body stretched out in front of her. From the chiseled shoulders that narrowed to firm hips, there wasn't a flaw on her body. Her ass cheeks were beautifully rounded and hollowed on the bottom as they connected to her thighs. Her thighs were arced to perfection, not large, but solid and in perfect symmetry with her upper torso. With proper nutrition and training, Marley could easily see Luna entering bodybuilding competitions and winning. There was no doubt Luna's body turned many heads, both male and female, and she had never hesitated to let her physical attractiveness seduce the woman of her choice at the bars, but she felt that Luna had grown beyond that woman. She watched the rise and fall of her body with each breath and found her hands eager to touch Luna. A change in the music brought Marley back to the task at hand. She checked the temperature of the oil and found it ready. She removed her robe, poured a portion into her hands and rubbed it into her palms as she approached the table. "I'm going to start at your neck and work my way down to your feet. Let me know if I use too much or too little pressure. It's not supposed to hurt. Okay?"

"Yes, Boss."

When she touched Luna's shoulders, Marley felt the warmth of her body seep into her hands, and she began kneading deeply into the layers of muscles across her shoulders. "You've got a few spots that will take more pressure than I can generate with my hands. I need to use my forearms and possibly elbows. Is that okay?"

"Do what you do best Marley. I trust you completely."

Marley leaned into Luna's body with her forearm, her skin and muscles rippling under the pressure, eliciting a moan from Luna. "Everything okay?"

"That feels wonderful."

"We've just begun. By the time I finish with you, your legs will feel like rubber."

"Just remember I have to walk out of here unless you plan on keeping me for the night."

"That thought has crossed my mind once or twice."

"I'm putty in your hands. Literally," Luna chuckled.

Marley continued her progress and Luna fell silent. For a moment, she thought she may have fallen asleep until her hands reached Luna's ass and she moaned.

"Damn, that feels good. You can play with my ass anytime."

For the second day in a row, Marley smacked her client's ass. "Hush now and relax."

"That's not gonna make me relax, but I'll try to be still."

As her hands slipped down below Luna's ass, Marley could feel the heat radiating off her skin. Her hands slid down the firm muscles through the oil, feeling each muscle contract and relax with each stroke of her hands. Marley was amazed by the lack of hair on Luna, each movement flowed easily across soft, bare skin. Her eyes devoured each glorious inch of Luna's body.

When she worked down to Luna's feet, she walked over for more oil. "Do you have any never evers, you'd care to share with me?" She hoped to distract Luna while she massaged her feet.

"Hmm. I've never ever slept over at a lover's before."

"Never ever? Have you not had a long-term relationship?" She took Luna's left foot in her hands and began massaging and Luna failed to twitch or giggle.

"I've never been with anyone that I wanted more than a one-night stand with. Until now."

Marley's movement stopped.

"Don't stop. My feet aren't ticklish under your hands, and what you're doing is making me orgasmic."

Marley chuckled. "Now that's a new one. I don't think I've ever been told that."

"Lindy says you have magic hands, but they are stronger than magic, whatever that is, but I know I love having them on my body."

Marley finished with her feet. "Roll over for me please."

Luna complied with her request.

"Would you like a towel under your neck?"

"Only if it will help me see you better."

Marley nodded and rolled up a towel to place under her neck. Luna's eyes were shining in the dim light, sparkling wells of excitement and something more. Could it be love? She gasped as her eyes traveled down Luna's body to her small breasts. Her nipples were erect and begging to be kissed, but she would keep her focus to finish the massage she promised. She steadied her trembling hands and reached for Luna's right arm to continue the massage. Luna's eyes followed her movement, each loving stroke down her arm, then across her chest, carefully spreading more oil across her sensitive breasts and down her stomach. Marley could feel the tremors inside Luna's body as she caressed her abs to the base of her breasts. Her eyes fell to the neatly trimmed patch of hair between Luna's thighs. So, she's not entirely hairless. She felt her lips curl up in a grin. "I have to ask if you wax or shave your body? You have so little hair."

"It's mostly the native-American blood in me. I do have to shave my armpits every once in a while."

"Lord, I wish I didn't have to shave. If I go too long, I could easily be mistaken for Big Foot."

"Naw, your feet aren't big enough."

"They keep me upright, so I reckon that's all that matters."

"I never knew a massage could feel this good, or I wouldn't have waited so long to ask for one."

"Well, I was serious about setting you up on a regular schedule. It does the body and mind good to be relaxed."

"You'll get no argument from me, ma'am."

"That's what I like to hear."

Luna locked eyes with Marley, "Since we've taken care of one of my never evers, what is one of yours?"

"Hmm, let me think."

Luna watched her with anticipation hoping it would be something sexual as that was what she did best, besides physical training. The focus on Marley's face changed to a grin and Luna knew she had thought of something.

"Well, I've used a strap on before as a giver, but never a receiver. I would trust you enough to be my first."

Luna was overjoyed at the statement. She used a strap on frequently with her customers and would ensure Marley's first experiment was pleasant and highly enjoyable. "I do believe I am qualified to fill that request, ma'am."

"I do too."

Luna watched as a blush filled Marley's face. "I promise I'll be gentle and make it an enjoyable experience for you."

Marley nodded but remained silent as she worked down Luna's legs.

"I was thinking maybe when we're done here, we could spend a little time in the sauna for a good sweat."

"That's not a bad idea. Then we could shower and relax the rest of today. I think it is time we ordered some Chinese take-out for dinner. We haven't done that in a while."

"Sounds wonderful."

Marley turned around and put on a robe and then handed one to Luna. "When you're ready to sit up, go slowly. You can put the robe on and go start the sauna while I clean up here."

Luna sat up on the side of the massage table. "Wow, you weren't kidding. My legs feel like they are rubber."

"There's no rush. Sit tight and I'll go turn the sauna on."

"Nope, just give me a second. I can do this," she grinned as she placed the robe over her shoulders.

"Just so you know, you'll probably be ready for a nap after the sauna drains the rest of your energy, but I don't think a nap will hurt either of us."

Luna ran a hand through her hair. "I think you might be right. I'm okay with that."

Marley began to clean up her work station and once Luna left the massage table, she sanitized it before taking the used linens to the laundry room. She turned off the warmer and music, then closed the door behind her as she started for the sauna.

Luna had just poured water over the heating stones when Marley arrived. "It's warming up."

"Fine, I'll set the timer for thirty minutes. I don't think we can handle more than that." Marley hung her robe on a hook and stepped inside. She climbed to the second level to allow Luna to stretch out on the bottom. "If you start feeling light-headed, we need to leave."

"It's okay. I snagged a bottle of water on my way here."

"Smart move."

Luna stretched out on the bottom row using a towel for a pillow. "This feels good already."

"You can sweat out any toxins you might have left in your body."

"Uh huh, that too."

Luna's voice sounded sleepy and when she looked down, Luna's eyes were closed. Such a wonderful view. She laid her head back and allowed the heat to cover her body. She could feel the sweat beginning to trickle down her sides and played her fingers across her abdomen. She still had a bit of the massage oil on her skin and it helped to bead the water. She glanced down to find Luna's body glistening with a mixture of oil and sweat covering her body. Marley closed her eyes and relaxed.

When the timer dinged, the light inside the sauna turned off. She looked down and was certain Luna had fallen asleep. She climbed down and gently shook her shoulder. "It's time to hit the shower sleepyhead."

"Wow, that half hour flew by." Luna sat up slowly, the sweat dripping from her body. "I definitely need a shower, but that felt really good."

"Come on then and we can shower and climb into bed."

"I'll stop by my flat to shower and meet you in just a few minutes," Luna told her as they started to climb the stairs.

"I'll leave the door unlocked in case you finish before me."

"See you soon." Luna slipped inside her flat.

Marley entered her flat and went directly to the shower. She slipped the robe from her body as she started the water. What a day. She closed the door behind her and enjoyed the luxury of a long shower. The water pelted her skin, with a gentle pulse which added to her relaxed state. She found herself looking forward to a nap and possibly for something more after they awoke. Dinner for sure, but maybe it was the time she and Luna became intimate. She would let nature take its course and not press the issue. There was no need to rush, but she was looking forward to the experience.

†

Luna's shower did little to invigorate her. In fact, it only made her yearn for a nap more. She dried and dressed in a tank top and a pair of cut off sweats. Not her most attractive outfit, but she really didn't own any sleepwear. Hopefully, Marley wouldn't mind. The door was unlocked and when she entered, Marley was just emerging from the bathroom, dressed in a t-shirt and a pair of boxers.

"I don't know about you, but that shower kinda did me in. I'm so ready for a nap."

Luna nodded. "I'm glad it's not just me. I thought the shower may perk me up a bit, but it just relaxed me more."

"Come then and let me snuggle into that hot body of yours." Marley held out her hand and led Luna to the bed. "I'm fine if you want to sleep naked. I know you don't do clothes well."

What the hell. She's seen every inch of me now. "Thanks. I feel like I'm tangled up when I wear something to bed." Luna slipped the sweats down her body and pulled the tank top over her head.

"I'd rather be tangled up with you." Marley dropped her boxers and pulled her t-shirt off. She drew back the covers and allowed Luna to climb in ahead of her.

Luna held up the covers until Marley climbed into the bed, and then pulled them over their bodies. "Come get tangled up with me."

Marley rolled onto her side and draped her leg between Luna's as she placed her head on her shoulder, her arm slung across her waist. "Is this comfortable for you?"

"Most definitely." Her hand played through Marley's hair as she settled in.

"Are you always this warm?" Marley purred as she snuggled into Luna.

"Pretty much. The massage and sauna got me warmed up too."

"I didn't think to set an alarm. Should I?"

Luna chuckled, "No, I won't sleep more than a few hours, if that. My body isn't used to sleeping during the day."

"Normally I'd say the same, but this last month or so has been pretty hectic getting the club up and running."

Luna softly stroked her hair. "It has been a wild time, but I think we've done better than Lindy even expected."

Marley's fingers stroked across Luna's abdomen. "She seems very pleased so far. I'm proud of the performance of the staff. Everyone is excelling at their roles and the ladies seem to be enjoying the extra attention."

"Do you think that will remain a high priority? The extra services?"

"I think it will peak and then settle down some. I don't think you have to worry about not staying busy though. You are definitely a crowd favorite."

"The extra money is nice, but I won't get into a habit of banking on it. The salary alone is better than I ever dreamed of making."

"I think we've all realized we've got it good here. I've learned so much from Lindy on running a business."

"Do you think she was serious about opening another club one day?"

Marley turned her head to look into Luna's eyes. "I'm not sure. It would be hard to duplicate the success, but Atlanta is a big city with a lot of prominent families. I guess only time will tell." She closed her eyes and listened to the beating of Luna's heart.

Luna felt Marley's body relax and knew she had fallen asleep. She closed her eyes and dreamed of Marley's hands on her body.

CHAPTER ELEVEN

Marley felt the rumbling in Luna's stomach as she woke from her nap. She glanced over at the clock to find it was nearing seven. *I guess we both needed a long nap.* Her lips curled into a smile as she looked into Luna's face. So relaxed and beautiful. Her fingers ached to stroke down Luna's jawline, but she didn't want to wake her peaceful sleep. *I wonder if I can sneak out of bed to order some food.* She slowly lifted her leg to roll away from Luna, and when Marley's weight was off Luna's body, she turned onto her left side and snuggled into a pillow. Marley crept from the bed and pulled a robe on as she grabbed her wallet and headed downstairs. She would call in the order from her office and wait downstairs for the delivery.

†

Luna felt a difference in the bed and woke to find Marley had moved. She no longer felt her snuggled into her. She reached behind her to find Marley's side of the bed empty and cool. She rolled over to find the flat was quiet and wondered where Marley had gone. She stretched and relaxed as her eyes scanned the room. She had never really paid attention to Marley's home before. There were a few photographs of her brother's family, but nothing more that gave away much of Marley's past. No photos of her with other women or even a group photo. She realized how little she knew about Marley and hoped that in the near future that would be changing. After several minutes elapsed and Marley hadn't returned, Luna got up from the bed and collected her clothes before walking into the bathroom. She relieved her bladder and slipped on her clothes. She ran some warm water in the sink and washed the sleep from her face. As she reached for a towel, her eyes came to rest on a bottle of perfume. Her fingers closed around it and lifted it to her face. She breathed in the familiar scent and felt the smile forming on her face. She replaced the bottle and ran a hand through her hair as she looked in the mirror. Not too bad. Luna left the bathroom and walked to the door to go downstairs in search of Marley. She opened the door just as Marley arrived carrying a large bag of food.

"That's perfect timing," Marley said as she walked past her into the flat. "The take-out just arrived, so I hope you're ready for a feast."

"Don't ya know it. I can always eat."

"Grab some plates and pour us a drink and I'll set the food out on the counter." Marley continued into the kitchen and began taking containers out of the bag.

Luna let out a moan as she walked past going to the cabinet, "That smells terrific."

"I tried to get a variety of dishes."

"It looks perfect." Luna sat two plates on the counter and opened a drawer for utensils. "What do you want to drink?"

"I think I'll have some iced tea."

"That does sound good." Luna poured them glasses of tea and joined Marley at the counter to fill her plate.

As they sat at the small table, Luna couldn't help but grin as the front of Marley's robe fell open while she ate. Marley hadn't noticed and Luna sure wasn't complaining about the view. The food was fantastic, but it wasn't what Luna had on her mind. She was eager to feast on Marley's body. She examined the delicate hands that had earlier brought her to the edge of orgasm with gentle kneading and deep caresses. *She is so amazing.*

"You sure have fallen quiet. Is everything okay?"

"I'm enjoying this feast. I didn't realize I was hungry until I got a whiff of the food."

Marley popped a piece of chicken into her mouth. "It is delicious."

She was the first to push her plate away. "I can't eat another bite."

Luna grinned and stabbed the last stalk of broccoli from Marley's plate. "I'm done too, and we have enough left over for at least one more round of meals."

"You definitely can't complain about their portions. The pricing is amazing too for this amount of food. It's an even better bargain when they deliver."

"I'll rinse these dishes if you'll place the leftovers in the fridge," Luna offered.

"You have yourself a deal, Ma'am." Marley began sealing the containers and carried them to the refrigerator.

Marley disappeared into the bathroom and Luna could hear the sound of her electric toothbrush. "I'll be back in a few minutes," she called out and left the flat. She walked into her flat and headed for the bathroom. After brushing her teeth, she slipped her shorts off and positioned the strap on harness around her hips. She found the dildo she planned to use with Marley and placed it securely on the mount. She slipped her shorts back on, positioning the dildo along her leg and placed a tube of lubricant in her pocket. She was smiling as she walked back into Marley's flat to see her brushing her hair in front of a full-length mirror just inside her bedroom.

†

Marley watched Luna enter the room and step up behind her. She felt strong arms encircle her body as Luna wrapped her arms around her from behind. Marley had pulled her hair to the left to brush it and Luna took advantage of the bare neck to bury her face in Marley's warm skin.

Luna breathed in deeply, "You smell delicious." Her lips kissed softly down Marley's neck.

Marley felt Luna's warm breath on her skin and her lips set her desire aflame. She felt a rush of moisture between her thighs. *Damn, she is so sexy. A simple kiss has me so turned on.* "That feels fantastic."

Luna's breath caressed Marley's ear, "I hope to make you feel completely satisfied."

Marley's hands fell silent as she allowed her body to enjoy the sensations Luna's lips were sending her. "I have no doubt you will."

†

Luna's hands slipped open the belt on the robe and it fell open, allowing her hands to caress down Marley's front,

172

making long strokes down her soft skin. She stepped closer as Marley leaned back into her body. She had no doubt Marley could feel the pressure of the mount against her ass as their bodies pressed together. She heard a soft gasp as her hips ground into Marley. She raised her hands to gently cup Marley's breasts, her nipples erect in anticipation. Luna rolled them between her finger and thumb as her mouth sucked Marley's ear lobe into her mouth. She felt Marley's hips rock back into her and when she looked into the mirror, she found Marley's eyes glassy with desire. The mirror gave her a perfect view of Marley's body. She slipped the robe off her shoulders and kicked it from between them on the floor. "So beautiful," she whispered as she planted soft kisses down her neck. Her right hand glided down her body and came to rest on top of her. She could feel the heat and moisture escaping Marley's body as her hand cupped her mound, squeezing gently, making Marley moan. She slipped a finger between silky lips and stroked slowly through the growing wetness.

"That feels so good," Marley growled.

Luna teased her entrance with slow strokes and she could feel Marley pressing her hips forward urging her to enter her. Her thumb stroked across Marley's clit and she groaned loudly in pleasure. "Spread your legs for me."

Luna felt Marley's movement as she exposed herself, opening her legs to shoulder width. She could feel a trembling in Marley's wetness as her fingertip probed inside. Marley was hot and wet with need, but Luna wanted to make sure she was relaxed and well lubricated before she introduced her to the strap on.

✝

Marley felt the harness and the dildo attached to it pressed against her and her hands grabbed Luna's shorts and pulled her closer. She could feel the firmness of the dildo through the soft fabric and the image of Luna thrusting into her made her heart pound with excitement. She felt her breathing quickening as her hips rocked into Luna. She couldn't believe how incredibly turned on she felt, her every contact with Luna's body sending waves of pleasure coursing through her.

Luna moved from behind Marley to stand in front of her and leaned down to kiss her. Her hands kneaded her breasts as Marley's tongue hungrily entered her mouth. Marley broke the kiss after several heated minutes. "I need you to make me come."

Luna's response was a smile as she turned Marley's body pressing her against the wall and she knelt in front of her. She spread Marley's legs and placed her left leg over her shoulder, exposing her center to her eager mouth. She leaned forward, planting soft kisses on Marley's center as she leaned back on the wall for support. Her tongue probed into the depths of Marley's vagina, her teeth grazing sensitive spots as she thrust her tongue deeper inside. Her face was coated with juices as she felt the first waves of pleasure crash through Marley and felt her hands grab her hair and pull her mouth tighter against her.

Marley cried out, "Oh, fuck yes, Luna." She was thankful for the support of the wall behind her. Her legs felt weak as the orgasm rocked her body. Luna kissed her mound softly and then rose to take her in her arms. She could feel the tremors in Marley's muscles as she pulled her close.

Marley felt weak, but her orgasm made her hunger for more of Luna. "You have way too many clothes on." Her hands pulled the shirt over Luna's head and then pushed the shorts down her hips. Luna kicked them away and the dildo pressed between Marley's thighs. The heavy silicone toy brushed across her lips as Luna kissed her and slowly rocked their bodies together. "I want you to fuck me, Luna."

Luna was surprised by the pleading tone in Marley's voice. "Are you sure you're ready?"

"I am more than ready. I want to feel you inside me."

Luna nodded and led her to the bed. "Lay on your back and lift your hips so I can put a pillow under you."

Luna placed the pillow under Marley's hips then retrieved the lubricant from her shorts pocket. She heard a soft laugh from Marley.

"I'm not sure you need that. I am so wet."

"Yes, you are, but I won't risk a dry toy hurting you. I want this to feel good for you."

She nodded and watched as Luna's hand coated the toy with the lube. She smiled as Luna approached the bed.

Luna lay beside her and her hand stroked down Marley's body as she leaned in for a kiss. "Promise to stop me if you don't feel comfortable, okay?"

Marley smiled. "Stop worrying and fuck me, silly."

Luna positioned her body between Marley's legs. The toy lay atop her mound and Luna took the shaft in her hand and ran the tip up and down the length of Marley's lips. Marley reached down to part her lips and Luna placed the tip of the toy inside her entrance. She shifted her weight and leaned forward above Marley as the dildo slid slowly into her. She looked into Marley's face watching for signs of discomfort, but all she saw in her eyes was excitement.

Marley felt inch after glorious inch glide slowly into her, moving smoothly as Luna's hips pressed into her. She felt her muscles relax welcoming Luna deeper into her. She couldn't keep her hands off of Luna. She caressed down her back to her ass, feeling the flexing of her muscles as she drove the toy deeper into her. When Luna was buried inside her, she could feel the heat from her skin seeping into her as they were mound to mound. She felt so pleasantly full with Luna's weight resting on her hands as she looked into her eyes.

†

Luna felt the toy sink to its full length and felt Marley's skin next to hers. She waited for several seconds to allow Marley to relax and then began a slow rhythm with her hips. "Music on," she called out and a cd of tantric music began to play, a gentle beat at first, building a rhythm faster and faster, allowing Luna's movement to match the music as it built to a crescendo. Marley's hips rose with each thrust of Luna's hips as they locked eyes and were lost to everything but the growing passion between them. A bead of sweat ran down Luna's back as she thrust deeply into Marley and when her legs wrapped around her hips, she knew Marley's orgasm was seconds away. She thrust wildly one last time and Marley groaned loudly as her hands gripped the sheets, her orgasm making her body quake in pleasure.

Luna was at the edge of orgasm when Marley exploded, but she was unable to come watching the pleasure roll across Marley's face. She slowly withdrew the toy and rolled over to the side of the bed. "Get up on your knees."

Marley cocked an eyebrow but moved into position, her hips just off the side of the bed.

Luna placed the toy at her entrance and slid deep on the first thrust. "Oh damn, you feel so good," she groaned as her hands locked onto Marley's hips.

"Damn… that feels good. Fuck me, Luna."

†

Marley could feel Luna's hips slapping her ass as Luna thrust into her, penetrating even further, her body still reeling from her orgasm. She never imagined anything could feel this good, but Luna hit every one of her erogenous zones with her movements. She listened to Luna's breathing becoming ragged and she knew Luna was close to climaxing. "Come with me baby," she cooed.

The sound of Marley's voice spurred Luna into a primal zone she had rarely ventured into as her hips pounded into her lover. Her legs were growing weak as her energy moved to her core and her body exploded. She cried out just as Marley screamed and they collapsed on the bed. Luna used the last of her energy to roll off Marley carefully withdrawing the toy. She was gasping for breath as she turned to look at Marley.

Luna unfastened the harness and lifted her hips to remove the strap on from her body, lowering it onto the pile of clothing on the floor.

Marley moved to lay her head on Luna's shoulder. "That was fantastic."

"I rather enjoyed it myself," Luna grinned.

Marley's fingers trailed down the front of Luna's body from her chin to her navel. "I just thought your body was perfect before, but in motion, it's even more beautiful."

"I'm glad you approve ma'am."

"I can see why the ladies rave after a session with you." Marley watched Luna's brow furrow. "Did I say something wrong?"

"With them, it's just a service. With you, it was something special for me." She shifted slightly to look Marley in the eyes. "If this was going to be my one time with you, I wanted it to be memorable for both of us."

"It was very memorable, and it won't be the last time."

Luna smiled and pulled Marley in for a deep kiss. "You don't know how long I've waited to hear those words from you."

Marley rolled on top of Luna. "I shouldn't have made you wait so long." Her lips caressed Luna's face. "I hope to make that up to you."

"You won't get any argument from me." Luna's husky voice vibrated against Marley's lips.

Marley made love to Luna with intensity, bringing her to several climaxes over the next hour then collapsed in her arms. She snuggled into her and they slept for several hours, bodies entwined and smiles playing across their faces.

†

The music was still playing when Marley woke and crept from the bed to empty her bladder. When she returned to the bed, Luna was awake and stretched out on her side. Marley grabbed a bottle of water and took a drink, then handed it to Luna. "Hungry?"

"I could eat. We've burned a few calories tonight."

Marley chuckled. "Yes, we have."

"Leftovers?" Luna asked with a smile.

"Sounds perfect to me." Marley located her robe and put it on while Luna found her shorts and T-shirt.

After finishing the leftovers, they snuggled on the couch and watched a movie until Marley couldn't keep her eyes open. "Let's hit the sack," Luna suggested.

Marley didn't offer any resistance when Luna took her hand, pulled her up off the couch and led her to the bed. She removed Marley's robe and shed her clothes before climbing in behind her, snuggling up to Marley's back. "Sweet dreams," she whispered and kissed Marley's neck.

"You too," Marley's sleepy voice answered as she pulled Luna's arm over her waist.

†

Luna stretched and her eyes popped open when she felt the warm body lying next to her. Marley was curled on her side still asleep, allowing Luna to watch her. Her chest rose with every slow breath and her lips twitched with a smile. *You are so perfect.* Tempted to reach over and brush a stray lock of hair from her face, Luna fought off the urge choosing instead to enjoy the precious moments before Marley woke and the calm would be destroyed with words. She breathed in the scent of her hair, the soft musky smell of their lovemaking warming on her skin. Marley sighed in her sleep and her eyes began to flutter open. When she looked into Luna's face, she opened her mouth to speak. Luna quickly covered her lips with a finger, then replaced it with her lips. She wrapped Marley in her arms and held her tight as they kissed. Luna deftly rolled Marley on to her back and began to kiss down the front of her body, her lips and hands burning a trail of desire as her head disappeared between Marley's thighs. Her tongue swirled inside Marley's entrance, causing her hips to rise from the bed eager for a deeper kiss. Luna felt the smile grow and then buried her face in Marley's silky wetness.

Marley exploded in orgasm and gasping for breath, managed to reach for Luna's face and pull her up. Luna rolled onto her side, smiling at her. "You're so pleased with yourself, aren't you?"

"A fine good morning, errr afternoon to you, Dear."

"Afternoon?" Marley lifted her head to look at the clock. "I can't believe we've slept this late."

"Me either. That was one of the best night's sleep I've ever had, and to wake up next to you was glorious."

"Do you always wake up this sweet?" Marley grinned up at her.

"Umm no. Usually, I'm rather sluggish in the morning from tossing and turning, but I don't think I moved at all last night."

"That wake-up call. Wow, let's just say a woman could get used to that."

"Could you?"

"I could indeed." Marley reached over to stroke Luna's face.

Luna pressed her cheek into Marley's hand. "I could wake up next to you every day."

"How would you feel about a shower and grabbing something to eat? We still have time to look at some vehicles today. Maybe after, we could stop off at Sister's for a drink before coming home."

"Home. That sounds good to me."

Marley sat up in bed. "I definitely need a shower."

"We both do." Luna stood and offered her hand to Marley.

CHAPTER TWELVE

Luna peered into the window of a sleek black Rubicon Jeep.

"You would look great behind that wheel."

She turned to Marley. "You really think so?"

"Irresistible. Not that you aren't already, but this Jeep would be the icing on the cake."

Luna pulled out her phone and took a photo of the window sticker. "I think this is the one." She grinned at Marley. "Ready to pick out your Land Rover?"

"I've already taken a peek at what they have in stock. I've narrowed it down to Midnight Black or Sky Blue."

"Well let's go check them out."

✝

Luna was tickled when Marley decided on the black. "I guess we have some wheeling and dealing to do with Danna."

"I think I'll let you do the negotiations. She has a rather soft spot for you." Marley chuckled.

"Does that bother you?"

Marley reached for Luna's hand. "Not in the least."

Luna's face turned into a frown, "You know I think there's something I need to share with you before we move on." She turned to face Marley in the seat. "There's something that's been bothering me about your comment about me being a one and done type person and I need you to understand why."

Marley hung her head. "I know that was a pretty insensitive thing for me to say. I'm sorry that I've hurt your feelings."

"You were spot on about my reputation, but not the reason why I have been that way. When I was twenty, I met a woman ten years older than me when I was out clubbing. At first, I thought she was just flirting with me but as the night wore on, she asked me to go home with her. I was still young and even though I'd had a few one-night stands, I didn't recognize the signs of a master manipulator." Luna ran her hand through her hair, a habit she had when she was stressed or nervous. "Melissa had it all. She was beautiful, a successful businesswoman, lived in a gorgeous home in Buckhead and drove a flashy red sports car. I was driving a beat-up old truck and living in an apartment with three other women at the time. Common sense should have told me, I was way in over my head, but Melissa showered me with attention and expensive gifts for a week before asking me to move in with her." Luna lifted her head and Marley could see tears in her eyes.

"My friends tried to warn me about Melissa, but I thought I was head over heels in love with her and I turned a deaf ear to their warnings. Things were fantastic for about a month until one night, I came home from work to see a Hummer parked in the garage, next to her sports car. I opened the door and walked in through the kitchen and found Melissa in the arms of another woman. I looked at her and she stared back at me. I asked Melissa, what the fuck was going on, and she turned to me. Luna, she said, this is my partner Jill. She's just returned home early from a tour of duty in the desert."

Luna's hand stroked through her hair. "I stood there like a dumbstruck idiot when I realized I had been played."

Jill smiled at me. "So, this is the adorable play toy that's been keeping you company while I was away?"

Melissa must have seen the rage in my face as reality hit me. "You are more than welcome to stay. Quite frankly, Jill would be delighted if you did."

"That woman actually told you that?"

"Yeah. I guess she felt I was so desperate, that I had no other options." Luna took a deep breath. "I told them both to fuck off, went to the bedroom and packed what I could and left the rest behind. My heart and confidence were shattered. My old roomies took me back in and helped me lick my wounds and slowly recover from my experience with Melissa. Since then, I've trusted no one with my heart. Until now."

"Oh Luna, I'm sorry you had to go through that experience and at such a young age. No wonder you don't trust people with your affections. I'm so sorry for misjudging you."

"I should have been honest with you years ago and maybe you wouldn't have formed that impression of me, but it's a hard story for me to tell and few people know the details. Melissa used me for her own selfish desires. I was vulnerable and ripe for the picking. After that, I vowed I would never let anyone that close to me again."

Marley reached across the seat and took Luna's chin in her hand. "I can't promise you lavish gifts or a high-profile lifestyle, but I can hold your heart as tenderly as I can and give you all the love I have to offer." She wiped away the tears from Luna's cheeks. "Thank you for sharing that with me."

"I didn't want you to think that you were only a conquest for me. I've loved you for years, but it's taken a long time to build up the confidence to trust anyone after Melissa."

"That certainly makes sense. I hope I never do anything that will ever question our trust for one another."

"If I died today, I'd go out of this world a happy woman because of you. Not just for realizing there is an us, but also for the opportunity to work side by side with you at the club. It alone has been a dream come true."

"For all of us, I think. I still have to pinch myself from time to time."

"Me too. Let's go get a beer."

"Are you actually going to drink a beer?"

Luna grinned. "Probably not, but you never know."

Marley turned the ignition on. "You never cease to surprise me."

†

When they arrived at Sister's, Alex had also just arrived for her shift. She stepped out of a Porsche and strolled across the parking lot. "Someone is stepping up in the world fast," Luna said as she nodded toward the dark figure walking into the back door of the club.

"Definitely a nice ride." Marley reached for her hand. "Let's go get a drink."

Heads turned when they walked inside hand in hand and Alex grinned up at them from the bar. "Good afternoon ladies."

Marley returned her smile, "Hello again. How are you?"

"Doing well thanks."

"We couldn't help but notice your new ride," Luna grinned. "That's one fine car."

Alex looked up at her. "Danna has loaned me her late husband's pride and joy until I can save up enough for a Harley."

"I didn't realize you knew Danna," Marley smiled.

"We met here in the club." Alex picked up a towel and started wiping down the counter.

Luna's face lit with a smile, "A woman with excellent taste. When you get hooked up maybe the four of us can take a ride."

"I'd like that," Alex smiled back. She turned to Marley. "I am so indebted to you for giving me a job at TWC. Everything is working out between the two places and I would have been so bored just working at Sister's."

"We're the ones who should be thanking you for joining the team. You've brought so much experience with you, including how to do a proper Nuru massage," Marley answered.

"Now I'll be able to get that ride faster with the money I'm bringing in. But more importantly, I'll be able to help out my family."

"Speaking of your family, have you found a solution for your citizenship issue?"

Alex grinned. "Danna is helping out with that too. It won't be overnight, but it's a start." She picked up the rag from wiping down the bar. "What can I get you, ladies?"

Luna settled onto a barstool next to Marley, "A bottle of water for me, and a Coors Light for the lady please."

"Coming right up," Alex spun on her heel and began to fill their order.

Marley couldn't help but admire the fit of the jeans over Alex's tight ass. She looked back to find Luna smiling at her. "See something you like?"

"Nice, but not as nice as yours."

"Great answer," Luna replied and leaned in to kiss Marley.

Alex placed their drinks in front of them. "So, is this a new development between y'all? Are you together now?"

Luna looked at Marley who nodded and smiled. "Yes, we are a couple now."

"I know that will break the hearts of many of our customers," Alex stated.

"I'm sure everyone will be just fine. There's a new kid in town for them to flirt with," Luna grinned at Alex.

Alex shook her head, "I'm amazed at the number of offers I get on every shift I work. There's no way I have the energy to tackle them all even if I had the interest, especially with all the special services I offer at TWC."

Marley smiled at Alex. "Has Danna captured your heart?"

"That would be a very good possibility. She's an amazing woman."

"You're planning to stick around for a while then?" Marley asked.

"Atlanta seems to be a great spot to put down some roots."

"It's an awesome place, full of opportunity for those who are searching to improve their life. It's been great for me and has brought me to the woman of my dreams," Luna told Alex.

"Oh my, someone has been bitten badly," Alex said with a wink to Marley. "Congratulations, Ladies."

"Thanks. I feel like I'm a lucky woman to finally be able to see what I've been missing for years." Marley leaned into Luna. "I have to admit it still feels like a dream."

Luna bent her head and bit Marley's earlobe.

"Ouch," she cried out.

"Okay, that's no dream," Luna chuckled.

Marley laughed but warned Luna. "You just wait until we get home."

Luna wiggled her eyebrows. "I can't wait."

"You two are adorable," Alex said.

"You wouldn't believe the romantic words that ooze out of Luna," Marley teased.

Alex nodded. "Yes, I would. All I needed to see was the way you two look at each other. You look perfect together."

"Not perfect, but we're working on that." Luna placed a ten on the bar. "Drink up so you can take me home."

"Forget the rest of the beer. Give me a call later in the week, Alex. I'd like to talk to you about sharing the wealth a bit. Maybe you would consider doing some training sessions on what you learned at the Ranch."

"Will do Marley. Have fun."

"I plan on it," Marley chuckled and grabbed Luna's hand.

"See ya Alex," Luna called as Marley rushed her toward the door. She heard Alex laughing as they stepped outside.

†

Clothes began hitting the floor between heated kisses as they entered Marley's flat. They spent hours exploring one another's bodies at a leisurely pace. After sating their appetites, Marley lay snuggled in Luna's arms. She enjoyed cuddling in Luna's warmth, her head resting on Luna's chest, listening to the strong beating of her heart. "How are we going to play this tomorrow when everyone is back at work?"

Luna let her hand stroke down Marley's arm. "I think we should remain professional in front of our clients but be open with our co-workers, and Lindy of course. I doubt we'd be able to hide anything from them anyhow."

"I agree. I'm very proud to be with you, but I don't think we should flaunt our attraction in front of clients. Would it be selfish of me to tell Lindy we aren't ready for a threesome with her?"

"I was hoping you'd feel the same way. I want our time to be just us. At least for now. If you change your mind down the road, then so be it. Lindy will understand."

"Yes, I think she'll be disappointed, but will understand our new relationship. Maybe down the road if you're still interested." Marley snuggled back into Luna. "Are we going to be okay with each other providing services to the clients?"

"I can't promise I won't be jealous of them spending time with you, but as long as I know it's just business and I'm still in your heart, I'll be fine."

Marley's face turned up to Luna. "You are definitely in my heart. I love you."

Luna smiled at the words she'd longed to hear from Marley. "I love you too." She bent down and kissed Marley.

"Thank you for a fantastic weekend," Marley scooted down in the bed beneath the covers.

"It's just the beginning," Luna replied.

"Spoon me then until I fall asleep."

"I'll spoon you anytime." Luna chuckled as their bodies molded together.

†

Marley awoke snuggled into Luna's warmth. She couldn't resist running her fingers down Luna's abdomen, her fingers gliding over the ripple of muscles, her touch leaving a wake of gooseflesh as her lover began to stir.

"You don't know how long I've yearned for that touch," Luna whispered.

Marley looked up into Luna's eyes, "I've dreamed of you so many times." She shifted onto her side, propping her head in her hand. "I was so scared I'd fallen for you and it would only lead to a broken heart."

"I would rather die than hurt you. I've loved you for so long."

Marley leaned down to kiss Luna. "I'm glad our hearts have finally met." She smiled sweetly. "When I woke a few minutes ago, I had an idea running through my head. I think it may prove to be an excellent one."

Luna rolled over on her side to face Marley. "Do tell, my love."

"It's time to offer Alex more responsibility. She could be like a preceptor or something. I think she'd make a great trainer for the other less experienced staff who provide our special services."

Luna's face filled with confusion. "I thought you wanted to wait a bit longer."

"Originally yes, but I think she will bring a whole new level of skill to the club that would keep Lindy and several other members very satisfied."

Luna chuckled. "Let me read between those lines. Alex will keep Lindy so satisfied you won't need to be in a hurry to satisfy her desire for a threesome."

Marley frowned. "Is my motive that transparent?"

"Only to me, but I think it's a great idea. Not only will it benefit the club, but it will help Alex financially reach some of her goals by giving her a bit more money with the expanded responsibilities. Why don't you set it up? I think she's been living with Danna."

"How do you think Danna will respond? She might not like it if Alex is spending more time at TWC, or providing services to more of her friends."

"That can't be our concern. I would hope Danna would see the wonderful opportunity Alex has to make a lot more money. If she really loves her, I think she wouldn't stand in Alex's way."

"I'll talk it over with Lindy and see what she thinks about the idea. I know she really enjoyed the pseudo-interview when Alex gave her a Nuru massage."

"Ha! I bet she'll jump at the chance to take a lead role in training the other interested staff. Just from the short conversations we've had, I can tell she loves pleasing women as much as I do."

"Let's hit the shower and get this day started. Lindy will be here early this morning."

Luna rolled off the bed and held out her hand to her. "I'm just waiting on you."

†

Marley's first appointment wasn't until ten, so she completed some paperwork in her office. Several times she took a break to get something to drink, which gave her an excuse to walk pass the workout room to see Luna working with a client. Her heart fluttered at the sight of Luna's movement. She was beauty in motion, a light sheen of sweat making her skin glow as her muscles flexed and relaxed.

Pepper was wiping down some equipment and caught Marley's attention. She grabbed an armful of towels and walked out to the hall. "I'm so glad the two of you have finally come to your senses, Luna has been waiting on you for years."

They started walking down the hall to the laundry. "I was too afraid I'd just be another conquest and she would break my heart."

Pepper chuckled. "A few years ago, that may have been true. Luna has been hurt deeply before. I think the fact that you could resist her charms was intriguing to her and made her pay more attention to you."

Marley chuckled. "A temptation that was so hard to resist. I'm glad we took the time to become friends before we became lovers. There's so much more to Luna than her talent to please a woman and that drop-dead gorgeous body."

"I agree, and I think you'll find a deeply romantic woman now that you've moved beyond the physical attraction."

Marley felt her face flush. "She is definitely a romantic."

The front door opened and Marley's massage client walked in. "Good morning, Ladies," she announced when she saw Marley and Pepper.

"Good morning, Elizabeth. I've got room one set up for you when you're ready."

"Thanks, Marley, let me drop off my things and slip into a robe and I'll be right there."

Marley split off from them and walked into her office to look at her appointment calendar. Lindy was scheduled at two for an appointment. She was a bit nervous about the conversation she would have with her boss, but she felt certain Lindy would honor her wishes.

†

Marley finished the massage and was sanitizing the room when she looked up to see Luna leaning against the door frame watching her work. "Hey."

Luna returned her smile. "I hope you're hungry. I went for sushi and couldn't make up my mind."

"Tell me you didn't get one of everything," Marley teased.

Luna shook her head and chuckled. "No, but there is probably more than you, me, Haley and Pepper can eat."

Marley picked up the linens from her massage. "Remind me to never take you to the grocery store hungry. It would cost a small fortune." She watched the smile grow on Luna's face. "Let me drop these off and wash up and I'll meet you for lunch."

"Awesome. What do you want to drink?"

"I'll stick with water. Thanks for going for lunch. I was getting hungry."

"My stomach was growling so loud, Pepper turned up the music."

"Ha, you better go feed that beast then. I'll see you in a few."

Marley walked to the laundry and dropped the linens in a hamper, then returned to the locker room to wash her hands. She was smiling at herself in the mirror as she lathered her hands. One good thing about being a massage therapist, the oils kept her hands soft and smooth. She loved the feel of warm flesh under her touch. The ripples of

Luna's body made them feel on fire. *Yep, you're a goner.* Marley turned the water off and reached for a towel.

†

When she walked into the juice area, her eyes fell on a table covered with trays of sushi. "Oh, my word, you weren't kidding," she told Luna.

"Nope, I couldn't decide, so I got a little bit of everything. I did remember one of your favorites," Luna grinned. "A super cowboy roll, with steak and shredded lobster." She handed Marley the tray with the succulent morsels. "There are a few new items I've never tried that I thought we could test out. The chef put a few pieces together in a sampler."

"This looks fantastic." Marley took the tray and slipped into a seat at the table.

Haley was seated across from her. "Pepper and I've decided to let Luna be the one to pick out all of our lunches."

"She certainly did a marvelous job on this one," Marley replied and took a bite of her cowboy roll. She let out a deep moan and opened her eyes to find all of them looking at her. "What?"

The group broke out in laughter. "I think we'd all agree you just had a mouth orgasm."

Marley nearly choked and reached for her bottle of water. She took a long drink. "I'd have to agree. That taste was orgasmic."

Luna winked at her lover. "I'll make a note to order cowboy rolls more often."

"Oh, yes." Marley chuckled and took another bite.

†

193

Luna and Marley packed up the leftovers to take up to Marley's flat. "I guess we don't have to worry about what's for dinner," Marley said as they climbed the stairs.

"I could watch you enjoy sushi every day," Luna said as she placed the leftovers in the refrigerator. She turned around and took Marley in her arms. "That was almost like foreplay."

Marley chuckled. "That was a most enjoyable lunch. Thanks for ordering and delivering it for us."

"It was really good. Provides a lot of fuel for working out too."

"Maybe I ate too much then. I'd love nothing more than a nap right now."

Luna glanced up at the clock. "What time is your next appointment?"

"Lindy is coming in at two."

"Do you plan to talk with her about her request and adding more to Alex's role here?"

"Yes, the sooner the better."

"Are you nervous?"

"A little bit, yes. I hate disappointing Lindy after what she has done for all of us."

Luna leaned forward and kissed her forehead. "Relax, Lindy will understand."

"I sure hope so."

"I have an appointment in fifteen minutes, but you could nap for a half hour," Luna suggested.

Marley shook her head. "I think I'd better stay alert. I've still got some budget work that can keep me busy."

Luna kissed her softly and stepped back. "I'm going to brush my teeth and head back downstairs. I love you."

"I love you too," Marley answered and watched her walk into the bathroom. Marley busied herself making the bed they had left disheveled earlier that morning. She picked up a pillow and buried her face in Luna's scent.

Luna returned from the bathroom and kissed her. "I'll see you after my appointments. Good luck with Lindy."

"Thanks," she answered and walked into the bathroom. She heard the door close and picked up her toothbrush. "Everything is going to go as planned," she spoke to her image in the mirror.

†

Her watch alarmed on her wrist, notifying her she had ten minutes before her appointment with Lindy. She left her office and entered the massage room to turn on the warmer and light a scented candle. She had just turned on Lindy's favorite music when a light tap sounded on the door. She turned to find Lindy standing in the doorway.

"I hope you are getting ready for me. My body is in dire need of your magic hands."

"I'm all set. You want to change and I'll wait for you here?"

"I will be right back then," Lindy said and spun away from the door.

Marley took several deep breaths as she mentally rehearsed what she wanted to say to Lindy. She was pacing the room when Lindy returned.

"Are you okay Marley? You seem a bit tense."

"No, Lindy I'm fine. I was just waiting for you. Come on in and we'll get started."

Lindy closed the door behind her and slipped off the robe and handed it to Marley. Marley hung the robe as Lindy laid face down on the massage table.

"Do you have any trouble spots we need to work on today?"

195

"My neck seems unusually tight for some reason."

"I'll give it some special attention then. How was your weekend?"

"Busy, Jay Dub had several functions planned for us to attend. Those so-called social engagements are so stuffy. Luckily for me, some of the other members were also attending so we could sneak away for some girl chat."

"That doesn't sound too painful," Marley said as she filled her hands with warm oil and started massaging it into Lindy's shoulders. "Ooh, you are tight."

"Mmm-hmm, and your hands feel great. How was your weekend?"

"It was fantastic. Very relaxing and enjoyable."

"Is that a purr I hear in your voice?"

Marley felt her face flush and was glad Lindy couldn't see it. "I think you know me too well," she answered.

Lindy chuckled. "Well, you have been bringing me pleasure of all types for some time now. I should be able to read you."

"That you do. Luna and I had a great weekend together."

"Does that mean that you have finally taken the plunge?"

She chuckled. "You have a less than delicate way of putting things, but yes after a long talk, Luna and I made love this weekend. Several times if you must know."

"All I can say in my defense is it's about damned time. She adores you and I think you feel the same for her."

"I do, and I'm glad that I've finally realized what I've been missing for so long. She makes me feel so complete, among other things."

Lindy's body shook with her laughter. "I can definitely attest to the 'other things' you speak of. She knows how to please a woman." Lindy shifted her body. "So, does this mean that you're a couple?"

"Yes, I believe so. We went to a club last night and didn't stay long. We weren't interested in anyone there besides one another. We're going to take things one day at a time and see where it leads us."

"That sounds like a smart decision. I'm sure there are many broken hearts to see the two of you together. You are both very attractive women."

"Thanks," Marley said as she began to work on Lindy's neck. "You feel a bit out of alignment. Do you have a chiropractor who could do an adjustment?"

"I was thinking the same thing. Yes, I'll make an appointment when we are done here."

They fell silent while Marley finished the session. "Roll over for me and I'll work on your front side."

Lindy turned on the table. Marley had her back turned to her to refill her oil and she took a deep breath before turning back around. She was ready to discuss Alex and delaying the threesome. There was no need to hold back any longer. She must have been frowning when she turned back around.

"Marley, why are you frowning so? Is everything okay?"

"I'm sorry, Lindy I was just deep in thought. There is a couple of things I want to talk to you about."

"By all means, spit it out before you get permanent wrinkles," Lindy teased. "You know you can tell me anything unless you have plans to leave."

"Heaven's no. I love it here." Lindy relaxed a bit. She began caressing the oil into Lindy's skin. "Part of the conversation Luna and I had this weekend was about your desire to have a threesome."

"Oh, good lord, is that what you're so tense about? Don't let that stress you."

"It isn't that we are not interested in helping you fulfill that fantasy, it's just that we are so new together we aren't prepared to share one another with someone else. We want our time together to be just us for now. Does that make any sense?"

"It makes perfect sense, Marley, so relax. I have a bit of a confession to make to you."

"What?"

"Trust me, I've always had the desire to experience a threesome, and there are no others I'd rather share that with than you and Luna, but I'll admit I was manipulating the two of you."

"You were what?" Marley stopped massaging and looked into Lindy's eyes.

"I hope you will forgive me, but I knew making that request would make the two of you at least talk about the chemistry between you. I hoped my suggestion would bring the two of you together for the first time. I know both of you well enough by now to know you wouldn't go into that kind of situation blindly."

"Well, you were correct about that. Neither of us wanted our first experience together to be shared."

"Trust me when I say I'd still love to share that experience, but now is not the time. Do you think you can forgive me?"

"That is quite a relief to hear actually, and we both owe you thanks for lighting a fire between us."

"Honey, that fire was lit a long time before, I just added a bit of fuel to it."

The blush rose up Marley's neck to her cheeks. "You certainly achieved that."

"If and when the time ever happens, I will be a happy woman, but just having the two of you in my life is more than enough."

"Thank you, Lindy. You can't know how stressed we were about disappointing you after all you've done for us."

Lindy reached up to stroke Marley's face. "The two of you have made me a happy woman again. I owe you so much more than you'll ever know. This place is beyond a dream come true for me, and all the other members."

Marley moved to lean on the edge of the bed. "There is something else, I'd like to suggest. Since Alex has started, more of the women are asking specifically for her because of her skill with Nuru massage. Remember how we tried to implement that technique and just having the supplies wasn't exactly cutting it?"

"Yes, I remember that. I know I enjoyed my time with her. I am still a little concerned about her immigration issues."

"Danna is helping her out with that. I think it is time to consider giving her an expanded role at TWC. Not only has she perfected the Nuru massage, but she has some knowledge in some other very specialized techniques."

Lindy cocked an eyebrow. "Do tell."

"While working at a brothel in Nevada, in addition to learning about Nuru massage, she also discovered something called a Yoni massage. From everything I've researched, I think that would be a huge success here. It doesn't hurt that she's tall, dark and handsome either."

"Like Luna?"

"Similar, yet different. I think the ladies here would be very pleased with a new offering."

"Can you arrange for a meeting so we can discuss this with Alex?"

"Just tell me when and I'll make it happen?"

"Tomorrow afternoon if possible. Jay Dub's going to Washington tonight."

"I'll do my best to make it happen. Will you be staying around after your appointment today?"

"I'd like to soak for a bit before showering and going home."

"I'll make a call then and see what I can arrange."

"Perfect," Lindy answered and closed her eyes for the final portion of the massage.

When she was finished, Marley pulled the sheet over a very relaxed Lindy. "All done, take your time and I'll check in with you before you go."

"Thanks, Marley," Lindy answered and Marley slipped out the door.

She walked down the hallway to find Luna finishing a routine with one of the other members. When Luna looked up to see her, Marley nodded toward the door. Luna nodded and turned back to her client.

"You did great today. See you on Wednesday?"

"Yes ma'am," the woman answered.

"Great, enjoy the rest of your day."

"Oh, I plan to. I have an appointment with Pepper in an hour upstairs."

Luna chuckled and walked toward Marley. "What's up?"

"I need to call Alex and arrange a meeting. I should probably have her number memorized after all the last-minute calls, but I don't. Thank God she finally got that cell phone."

Luna laughed. "Yeah, she finally entered the twenty-first century. I'm sure we have Danna to thank for that. Did it go well with Lindy?"

"Yeah, it did. She's going to soak a bit, but wants us to set up a meeting with Alex tomorrow afternoon if we can."

"Okay, let me pull out Alex's file with her cell number and I'll meet you in the office."

"Thanks. By the way, you look delicious."

"I'm smelling a bit ripe. You up for a soak later?"

"You bet."

"I'll see you in a few minutes then," Luna returned to the gym to track down Alex's number.

Marley went to her office and sat at her desk. She admitted to herself she was excited at the possibility of Alex expanding their services. Her presence would allow Luna some relief when it came to providing services to the ladies upstairs. Luna truly enjoyed her work, but the first few weeks after the club opened, she was exhausted from all the extras provided to the new members. The extra activities had slowed some, but it was still a physical strain for her.

Luna walked into the room and handed her a note. "Here's Alex's cell phone number. I'm sure we'll be able to get ahold of her in time. Hopefully, she's adapted to having a cell phone enough that she never leaves home without it."

"I hope so. I'd like to have this set up before Lindy leaves."

"Umm, did you update Lindy on Alex's immigration issues?"

"She doesn't know the detail. I told her Danna was helping to resolve the issues. I think I'll ask Danna to talk to Lindy and maybe she can set her mind at ease."

"That's a good idea. Let me know how I can help. I've got another appointment, but pull me if you need me."

"I think I can handle this."

Luna stepped in for a kiss. "I'll be back for more of those."

†

Marley picked up the phone and dialed Alex's number. She floated the idea of having a meeting to talk about a possible expansion of her role and the services at TWC. Alex seemed thrilled with the possibilities. She mentioned needing to check with Sister's first, but tentatively set up the meeting for eleven. Marley asked to talk to Danna if she was close by and then laid out her proposed plan for Danna to talk with Lindy about Alex's immigration status and what they were doing to resolve the issue.

Marley ended the call and slipped her cell phone in her pocket and walked to the Roman bath to update Lindy. She was excited about giving Alex more responsibility and wanted to clear her entire afternoon to spend at the club and begin to set everything up if the meeting went as well as she expected it to.

"We have a tentative meeting set up for eleven."

"Thanks, Marley. I know you are excited about this too."

"Yes, I am. I think the expanded and refined services will be a wonderful direction for the club."

Lindy sighed and sank deeper into the water. "She'll be perfect. I might have to experience this Yoni massage for myself."

"That she will." Marley walked back to set up for her next appointment. As she walked by the workout room, Luna was working with a member. Luna caught her eye and winked. "Damn, I'm one lucky woman," Marley said softly to herself and walked down the hall.

When she walked by the reception desk, Haley called out to her. "Your next appointment is running about fifteen minutes late."

"Thanks, Haley." As she started to her office, her cell phone rang. A smile lit up her face when she recognized the number. Alex had wasted no time checking with Janice. She pushed the button to accept the call. "This is Marley." She listened as Alex thanked her again for the interview and asked for details about the meeting. "There will be an opportunity for you to show off your talent to Lindy, so bring your 'A' game. I know you're a professional, so relax and do what you do best, and you'll be perfect. She already experienced the Nuru massage, so maybe you can show her the Yoni massage that I told her about. That's great, we'll see you tomorrow."

Marley walked back to the reception area. "Lindy will probably be gone by the time I'm done with my appointment, so please let her know everything is set for tomorrow. She'll know what I mean."

"Does this mean Alex will be spending more time here at the club?"

Marley smiled at her intuition. "Probably so, Haley."

"Awesome," she said and turned to answer the phone.

CHAPTER THIRTEEN

Marley finished her massage and sanitized her room. She was changing clothes to spend some time in the bath when Luna's upstairs client walked into the locker room with an extremely satisfied grin on her face. Marley returned her smile. "Have a great night."

"I doubt it could get any better. But thank you, Marley." She turned away and started the water for a shower.

I understand that completely. I'm ready for my next dose of Luna too. She pulled on a robe and walked down to find the bath empty. She slipped off the robe and stepped into the soothing water. The room was quiet, except for the gentle lapping of the water and Marley found herself completely relaxed. Her eyes were closed and she didn't see Luna entering the room.

Luna slipped off her robe and stepped into the bath. "You look very relaxed," she stated, causing Marley to startle.

"Oh, hey," Marley stammered as she wiped the water she had splashed from her face. "So relaxed, I didn't hear you enter. Are you done for the day?"

Luna lowered her body into the water next to Marley. "Yes, ma'am. It's been a long day and I'm very happy to end it soaking with you."

Marley could hear the weariness in Luna's voice. They had been working hard for several months and she knew the pace hadn't slowed much, especially for Luna. The women just couldn't get enough of her 'special attention', and now their relationship was adding to the physical exertion. She couldn't help but smile at the last thought. "I think it's time we have a quiet dinner and a relaxing evening alone."

Luna wiped the hair back from her face. "I won't argue with you at all. I'm worn out tonight."

"Let's soak for a little bit and we can shower, then I'll make us a nice salad for dinner."

"That sounds great. I think I worked off lunch about two," Luna grinned.

"You must be starved then. Do you want to eat first?"

"Nah, we'll stick to your plan. Do we have some meat to put on the salad?"

"Yes, Dear," Marley answered. "I planned on adding some grilled chicken slices. I know you need your protein."

"Thank you, my love," Luna answered and leaned in to kiss her softly. She stretched her legs out in front of her. "So, everything went well with Alex?"

Marley nodded, "Everything is arranged for tomorrow. All she needs to do is show up and work her magic. I already know she's excited about the prospect of expanding her role here."

"She'd be crazy if she wasn't. This place is amazing for many reasons. I have to admit, she's really added something to the club."

"I'll agree with you there even if I am a bit biased. I love it here."

Luna laid her head back and closed her eyes as they fell silent for a short while as the water caressed their tired bodies. She finally lifted her head and looked at Marley. "If we don't get out of here soon, I don't think I'll make it through dinner."

"Let's head upstairs then," Marley answered and stood in the shallow bath. She held out her hand to Luna.

†

After a quick shower, they dried off and donned clean robes. As they left the bathroom, Marley pointed to the couch. "Go relax and find us something to watch while I make our salads."

"You don't need my help?"

"Nope, I've got this covered."

"Thank you." Luna kissed her and walked to the couch. She picked up the remote and started surfing while Marley busied herself in the kitchen.

She prepared two salads, adding extra chicken to Luna's and called out to her. "Honey mustard or ranch?"

"Honey mustard, please. You sure you don't need my help?"

"Come get us bottles of water unless you want something else," she answered. She added the dressing to the salads and took out two bottles of water and handed them to Luna. "You can grab a couple of napkins too. I'll bring the salads."

"Wow, those look delicious."

"I hope they will be," Marley replied as she picked up the two large bowls filled with the chopped salads and followed Luna back to the living area.

When Luna swallowed her last bite, she stood and picked up the bowls. "You cooked, so I'll clean. Do you need anything from the kitchen?"

"Just you," Marley answered and relaxed back on the couch.

With a quick peck to Marley's forehead, Luna walked to the kitchen. She rinsed the dishes and placed them in the dishwasher. When she returned, she stretched out on the couch and relaxed in Marley's arms. "Is this comfortable for you?"

Marley pulled Luna's back into her chest and draped her arms around her. "This is perfect."

They relaxed, watching a sitcom together until Marley felt Luna's breathing deepen. She was so relaxed she was nearly asleep. She was enjoying the warmth of Luna's body tucked in close to hers and had given up on trying to follow what was happening on the television set. With Luna in her world, she was more than content with her life. She was excited to have someone to share her dreams. Luna was the perfect fit for her. She heard a soft snore escape Luna and stifled a giggle. She pulled her arms tighter around Luna and gave her a gentle squeeze. "Let's go to bed, Luna."

Luna's eyes popped open at the sound of Marley's voice. "Oh my gosh, I'm so sorry for falling asleep on you."

"I was about right there with you and decided we both needed to head off to bed. As long as I'm snuggled next to you, that's all I need."

They walked into the bedroom and Luna pulled back the sheets and removed her robe. "Do you want a sleep shirt?"

"No, I want to feel your skin next to mine," Marley answered as she dropped her robe and stretched out on the bed.

Luna climbed in beside her and kissed her sweetly. "I'm sorry, I'm so bushed tonight."

"Don't be. I'm perfectly content to be wrapped up in your arms."

"Turn off the light then and come here," Luna purred in a soft voice.

Marley reached over to turn off the lamp and rolled into Luna's arms. She laid her head on Luna's shoulder while draping an arm and leg across her body. "Good night, my love."

Luna stroked her hand down Marley's back. "Good night. Thank you for making my dreams come true."

She felt Luna relax as she drifted back to sleep. She buried her face in Luna's neck, breathing in her delicious scent and with a heart full of happiness, she followed her to dreamland.

Story continued in The Pleasure Workers
by Annette Mori
Release date September 1, 2019

THE PLEASURE WORKERS

CHAPTER ONE

Alejandra didn't feel like her name ever fit her. As soon as she earned the right to make a stand, she'd declared to her parents her preference for Alex. That name seemed to fit a whole lot better for reasons she'd never shared with her very Catholic parents. When she was growing up, her mama had wanted her to learn a more fitting vocation, something more suited to a woman, like nursing or teaching. Both were professions that contributed to society. Alex tried to remind her mama that even if she managed to get an education, she couldn't possibly work for a hospital or a school without a valid social security card. But the real reason was she didn't have an affinity to medicine or education, preferring to follow her papa around and learn all about fixing things.

Papa was her hero. Juan could fix everything. He could do anything. She wanted to be just like her papa and she was good at it too. She took to plumbing, electrical, painting, and all manner of machinery, like a duck to water. Her mama had given up well before Alex hit puberty and seemed resigned to what was clearly Alex's preference.

The wind kicked up again and the dirt swirled around her causing another round of uncontrolled coughing. As the truck approached and pulled onto the shoulder, the dirt tornado expanded. Her need to expel the foreign material from her lungs took on a new level of desperation. Alex liked giving her papa shit, so she'd joked with him on the afternoon right before everything came crashing down around her family and forced her into her current situation. That had been nearly eight long months ago. She was a desperate woman with no job, very little money, and no idea where to go. Not that she'd collected very much while living in Nevada, but for the second time in less than a year, she'd had to go on the run with little more than what she could carry in a pack on her back. A memory surfaced from the last conversation she'd had with her papa.

Her papa kept blowing his nose and complaining loudly as he tinkered with the small motor old man Hartford had brought in for him to fix.

"Hey, Papa, you should really find some triactin." Alex handed her papa a small screwdriver anticipating his need.

"Triactin?" Her papa scrunched his face. "Is that a new remedy, Mija?"

"Uh huh." Alex laughed. "Try acting like a man." She leaned back and held her stomach while laughing without restraint.

"Very funny, Mija. You should become comedian and stop following your old papa. You not laugh so hard if you catch this cold from me."

"Sorry, Papa. I couldn't resist. Mama always says how much the men complain when they get a tiny sniffle and how the women endure so much more. She says that's because it is expected of us."

"True, your mama endure a lot to bring your enormous body into world. At nine pounds, I thought surely she give me a son."

"Do you regret she could only give you one child and it was a girl?"

Juan reached over to pat Alex. "Never. You my pride and joy. So beautiful and talented. You take over family business when I die. It will expand. You not make the mistakes I have. I do not have good judge of character like you and mama."

Alex sobered quickly. "I'm sorry I couldn't handle all the work. I wish you didn't have to hire anyone else and then we wouldn't need to trust someone outside of the family."

Juan shrugged. "Price of success and fulfilling American dream."

"I suppose."

The truck skidded to a stop and Alex brought her face to the passenger side window as she peered in. The gapped tooth smile of a man with a deeply lined face studied her. He seemed harmless enough. Besides, at nearly six feet tall with well-defined muscles, Alex could easily fight her way out of a tight situation if she needed to. The man looked like a strong wind could blow him over, but it was always the small wiry ones she'd had to watch out for. The men who knew a hard day's work and spent the day in the hot sun were not to be taken lightly. Even though the owner of this beat up jalopy appeared to be in his 70's, he was one of those hard working types she'd known from hanging around her papa's friends. Most of the men worked the farms. She made a split second decision and tossed her ratty old pack into the back of the open truck.

"Where ya headed young man?"

"East." Alex wasn't about to correct his error. Sometimes she was mistaken for a guy. She could live with that, especially if it kept the assholes from hitting on her. She lifted her baseball cap off her head and pushed her fingers through the perspiration that had collected in her short thick locks.

When she pulled on the silver handle to open the door, the truck groaned and squawked at her, almost as if trying to communicate that like its owner, she was old and this sprite young'un ought to treat her with gentleness and care. Folding her tall lean body inside, she cautiously closed the heavy door and winced at the loud clang. The vinyl seats were covered with gray duct tape in an attempt to patch up the numerous cracks and tears in the upholstery. No air conditioning. Well, beggars couldn't be choosy. "Thanks for the ride. However far you can take me is fine with me."

The old man's eyes narrowed as Alex pulled the seat belt across her chest. "Oh, I'm sorry. I thought you was a fella. I suppose I shoulda looked closer. You sure don't have a man's face or uh, body." He coughed. "You ain't got nothing to worry about though. Been married to my wife for nearly sixty wonderful years. You know you shouldn't be out here hitchhiking. There's a lot of crazy people running around in the world today. Some that ain't so nice."

He offered his words of wisdom and Alex thought there was something sweet about him. She knew how shitty some men and women could be. This wasn't the first time someone had mistaken her for a boy, albeit a pretty boy, they had said. She'd gotten her full lips and high delicate cheekbones from her mama. Her papa had contributed her smoldering brown eyes that some had described as bedroom eyes. She was glad to have inherited them from her papa. Many a woman had fallen prey to her expressive eyes.

The low rumble of the engine played in the background instead of music as the old man pulled his ancient truck onto the rough road. Alex noticed a large hole where a radio may have resided long ago. She settled in as the engine's sound lulled her with the familiarity of riding inside an old jalopy.

"I'm pretty good at taking care of myself. Been doing it for a while now." The reality was that she hadn't always taken care of herself. She'd depended a whole lot on her family. It wasn't until she had to go on the run, that life had handed her a crash course in how to be an adult. Before that she'd led a sheltered life in her sleepy little town. Following her papa around and taking the evening meals with her mama and papa. She hadn't even felt the need to move out of her family home.

"Name's Henry," he grunted. His cheeks looked like an alien was moving around inside, before he turned his head toward the open window and spit out a sunflower seed.

"Alex."

Henry shook his head. "Just like my granddaughter. Had a perfectly good name, but said Georgiana don't fit her. Makes us call her George. I don't like it much cause it makes me think of those Bush's from Texas." He cackled. "You a lesbian, too?"

Alex raised her eyebrow. "If I answer honestly, will you still give me a ride?"

"Course. Love my granddaughter. She can't help how she was born. God don't make mistakes, ya know."

Alex smiled. "In that case, yeah."

Henry eased his truck back onto the road. "You single?"

Alex laughed. "Why? Is your granddaughter?"

"As a matter of fact, she is. But you ain't her type. She likes em a bit frillier. You know, them lipstick lesbians."

"Too bad. I don't have a type. I like them in all shapes, sizes, and styles. Never met a woman I didn't appreciate."

Henry grabbed a handful of sunflower seeds. "Me too and then my wife tamed my wild side. When you meet the right one, she becomes your type for life." Nodding, he shoved the seeds into his mouth. He pointed at the bag offering some as they traveled along the road kicking up more dust.

Alex declined his offer. "If you don't mind me asking, how far can you take me?"

"How far you need to go to get away from whatever you're running from?"

Alex stiffened in her seat. "A couple of hours on this road should do it. Maybe to a truck stop where I might be able to catch a longer ride. How'd you know?"

"I been on this planet for a lot of years. I reckon I know about stuff sometimes. It's the way people look around or carry themselves. I can tell when someone's a good person and hasn't had a fair shake in life. Never been wrong before and I don't 'spect I'm wrong now. I got just the place to drop you off. I might even know someone to give you that lift."

"Thanks, Henry. You remind me a little of my papa. Maybe my luck is changing and this is a sign." Alex turned away and looked out the open window. She didn't want Henry to see the tear that had formed and think she was soft or something. She suspected he knew but ignored her sudden flash of emotion. Yes, he was a lot like her papa. She was going to find a way to bring them back, no matter what it took. She figured Henry might see the resolution in the setting of her jaw, so she forced herself to relax and smiled at him.

†

Holy shit. Henry screeched into the truck stop, his tires leaving their mark along with the pungent smell of burning rubber. "Henry, I still have a lot of years ahead of me. Are you trying to kill us?" Alex placed her hands on the dash bracing herself as the truck skidded to a stop.

Henry pulled on the door and jumped out. "Come on, Alex, Rosie's getting ready to leave. Guess I got to jabbering too much and lost track of time." He began running toward an eighteen wheeler starting to ease out of the parking space the big rig had recently occupied. He was waving his hands madly in the air.

Alex thought for an old man, he was very quick. She was afraid the truck couldn't see him as the sky began to darken. She jumped quickly out of Henry's old beater and joined him in his waving routine. She winced when she heard the squealing brakes. A minute later a compact woman with short cropped salt and pepper hair jumped down from the cab. She placed her hands on her hips and frowned.

Alex didn't ever like to feed into stereotypes, but diesel dyke was what popped into her head and she mentally chastised herself. For an older woman, she was certainly attractive enough, but then again as Alex had told Henry, she didn't have a type. All women were appealing to her. Nothing compared to the sheer beauty of a woman reaching climax as she threw her head back in pure ecstasy. Alex lived for those moments. Although she'd had to discover those opportunities outside of the tiny town she'd grown up in, and lived most of her life before she went on the run.

"What the hell, Henry. I almost mowed you down," the woman said. As if the woman all of a sudden registered there was another person standing next to Henry, her eyes roamed across Alex's body. Alex felt like the woman was leaving no stone unturned as she checked out every inch of Alex's tall frame. Her eyes spent a few extra seconds on Alex's breasts and then a slow smile emerged on her face. "Who's your friend, Henry?"

"This is Alex. She's a sweet young gal who needs a ride east. I didn't want her accepting a ride from some low life, so I thought you might give her a lift."

"I sure can. Come on sweet thing. Grab your bag and I can take you as far as Atlanta. Name's Rosie." She took several steps closer and held out her hand. "Very pleased to meet ya."

"Um, I sure am appreciative of the ride, ma'am, but can you not call me sweet thing. I'm a bit more sour than sweet." Alex took Rosie's hand.

"Fair enough if you don't call me ma'am. I already feel old. I'll look forward to the company and the energy of someone on the younger side of life. Thanks for bringing a nice woman I can pass the time with, Henry. You give my best to your wife. Oh, and tell that adorable granddaughter I said hello. If only I was thirty years younger."

"You old cougar. You know she had a crush on you," Henry teased.

"Now you know you don't have to lay that bunch a malarkey on me. I'd be eager to give this handsome little gal a ride. She's definitely brightened my day." Rosie winked and her blue eyes twinkled.

Alex got a mental picture of Rosie's sapphire eyes darkened in arousal and she considered whether there was enough time or opportunity to finagle a way for her to experience that versus simply imagine the scene. She was good at two things—sex and fixing things. Her papa always said she should capitalize on her talents and not dwell on the things she wasn't very accomplished at. Especially cooking. When she was barely ten, she'd attempted to impress him with disastrous results. He'd kindly informed her she best leave the cooking to her mama, who was the only master in the kitchen they'd ever need. If Alex took away that joy, her mama wouldn't be utilizing the talents God bestowed on her. Juan insisted God had decided on a whole different set for Alex. Alex mused that if only her papa had known about her other skill set, he might not have encouraged her so much to find her niche in the world.

Alex's mama had different ideas about cooking. She had decided the importance of passing down their culture and her gift was more valuable than the numerous messes she'd have to clean up. Her mama never gave up and taught Alex how to make homemade tamales and a decent breakfast burrito. If that was the only authentic meal she could make, so be it. That skill might come in handy one day if she was trying to impress a woman. Besides, she got to spend time with her mama and that made them both happy.

Alex showed Rosie her gleaming white teeth as she offered her most seductive smile and then ran back to Henry's truck to retrieve her bag. Maybe this woman would appreciate being on the receiving end of her touch.

Pack in hand she grinned at her new friend and said, "Ready whenever you are." Turning to Henry she felt a rush of affection and dropped her pack, then pulled the wiry man into a bear hug. "Thanks for the ride, Henry. I won't forget you and your kindness. Will you give me your contact information? If you don't mind, I'd like to keep in touch and maybe someday find a way to repay you for picking up a stranger and giving me a reason to have hope for mankind after all."

"Dontcha worry about that, Alex. I was happy to have you come along when I saw ya on the side of the road. I'll give you my address. I like the idea of getting a letter from you. Knowing you've settled somewhere and things are looking up for you will make this old man's heart soar."

Rosie pulled a pad from the front pocket of her shirt and handed it to Henry. She began patting her pants pockets until she found a ballpoint pen that Alex figured she'd shoved into the back pocket of her jeans.

Henry grabbed the pen and started scribbling his contact information. "I guess you're always prepared, Rosie." He winked. "Ya never know when you're going to meet the one, huh? It'd be a shame not to have paper and pen to get their number."

Rosie smacked Henry on the arm. "Now ya know that ain't why I carry those things. Gotta jot down if my cargo has a problem on delivery. Boss man always wants the details and I write down exactly what the customer says, word for word."

Henry chuckled and handed Alex the paper he'd ripped off the pad, and then gave Rosie back her pad and pen. "I know, Rosie. I just like to tease ya. But ya know ya ain't getting any younger. When ya gonna settle down with a nice little gal who can have a meal ready for ya when ya come home from a long stint in the big rig."

A sad smile crossed Rosie's face. "Maybe someday, Henry, but I gotta convince the one I've had my eye on for years and so far, no luck."

"I'm rootin' for both of ya." Henry waved and returned to his old beater.

At least Alex got to say a leisurely goodbye to this man who reminded her so much of her papa. That wasn't a luxury she'd had when they took her mama and papa away. She tried not to let the melancholy get to her as the memory flashed before her eyes. A warm hand on her arm interrupted the sadness Alex felt. She quickly painted a smile on her face as she followed Rosie to the large eighteen wheeler in the middle of the truck stop waiting on them.

Alex looked up at the enormous vehicle with the bright yellow paint job. It reminded her of one of those cartoon suns—all bright and shiny. She liked the smooth round surface over the top of the cab and thought the rig matched the owner perfectly. Rosie had a broad smile on her face just like a ray of sunshine.

The next adventure was around the corner for Alex. She could feel it in her bones.

†

"So what's your story, darlin'? Not that I don't think you can't take care of yourself" —Rosie let her eyes once again roam over Alex's body— "with those rippling muscles and your impressive height, but why are you hitchhiking by yourself? Henry was right to bring you to the truck stop and catch me before my long haul to Atlanta. No offense, but there's a lot of ignorant rednecks lookin' to fuck up, um..."

"A Mexican dyke?" Alex shot Rosie a wry look. "Hey, don't worry about it. There isn't a lot of love for brown people, what with us all coming from shithole countries. I'm used to the slurs."

"Somebody chasing you or something? You don't have to worry about me. You can consider this truck a rolling, sanctuary city. I don't believe in that stupid wall or sending people back who lived their whole life here."

"What makes you think I wasn't born here?" Alex's jaw clenched and her tone had a clipped edge to it.

Rosie shrugged. "Look, I don't mean to rile you up or anything. I'd be sensitive too if the President started talking about the Irish like he talks about Mexicans. My grandparents came from the Emerald Isle. Immigrants who worked their asses off in the factories. None of us ever went to college, but I make a good living driving a rig. It suits me."

"Fixing things suits me, but it's hard to get a job without references. I've only ever worked in the family business and then on a kind of ranch in Nevada." Alex turned away and looked out the window. "I liked it there. Got to use some other skills, too, until...well turns out that no good deed goes unpunished. Felt bad about not giving my notice, but hey, it was time to leave."

"I can tell you're a good person, so if you're running, I suspect the jerk chasing you is some asshat that got his knickers in a twist for some shitty ass reason."

Alex returned her gaze to Rosie giving her an appraising look. "Thanks. I appreciate you giving me the benefit of the doubt. So who's the woman that captured your heart but hasn't seen the light?"

"A friend. She's Catholic and they don't get divorced. Married to a real son of a bitch. I've wanted to kill the bastard so many times but she won't let me intercede. She's afraid he'll take it out on their daughter. She's a grown woman now, so I don't understand why she won't let me help. Wish the fat bastard would keel over and die of a heart attack. I bring him food sure to clog his arteries every chance I get. The stupid asshole thinks I'm being nice."

Alex chuckled. "Keep it up and maybe you'll get your wish. Does she love you back?"

Rosie shrugged. "I think so. We haven't been, uh, intimate with each other, but yeah, I know she loves me in that way. I catch her looking at me sometimes and I know it's longing I see in her eyes. Some days I want to make love with her so bad, it nearly kills me not to touch her."

"So, then how do you, ya know, take care of your urges? Surely you aren't keeping yourself from having sex because she's a devout Catholic. Remember those skills I told you about, well I might as well confess that my last employer was Stacey's Ranch. They do a pretty good business and you'd be surprised how many women ask about having a sensual experience with another woman. I could help you release some of that tension. It's the least I can do since you're giving me a ride and all."

Rosie laughed. "No thanks. I'm an old fashioned kind of gal. I can't ever see myself making love with someone I'm not in love with. You're a very handsome, tall drink of water that I'm sure most lesbians would jump at the chance to bed. But, I'm not one of them. I'm not giving you a ride so's I can have myself a quick fuck, but thanks for the offer. Stacey's Ranch, huh? Never heard of it."

"Well, you know prostitution is legal in some parts of Nevada. The Ranch is like a high end spa that offers a few extras. Fifteen percent of their business is middle aged women wanting to check out whether they've been missing out on something all their lives. They aren't sure if they're a lesbian or even bi-sexual, so Stacey's is a safe place to explore. I was developing quite a clientele until one night someone followed one of my regulars. Her husband started beating on her. I wasn't going to let the bastard continue using her as if she was his own personal punching bag."

"Let me guess. He took one look at you and called in a few favors with his redneck buddies."

Alex nodded. "Worse. His brother was an INS agent. I got lucky because someone found out they were coming for me and tipped me off before they could make a grab. So now you know the whole sordid story even though I didn't want to tell you."

"Look, I didn't mean to pry. There's a lot of that going around and it was an easy assumption to make. Sorry about that. I'm no better than the rest when I start making guesses based on the color of your skin. Are your parents still alive and do they live in the states or were they rounded up as well?"

Alex turned away again. She looked down at the white lines in the middle of the highway after Rosie had changed lanes and began to pass the slower eighteen wheeler. She tried to let them hypnotize her into a state of calm. She didn't want to open that old wound. So far she hadn't made enough money to pay the exorbitant fees to help them cross the border again and start a new life somewhere else. "I'm guessing they're in Mexico right now and not doing so well. Can we talk about something else?"

"Sure, sure."

ABOUT THE AUTHOR

ALI SPOONER

Ali Spooner, a native of Florida, is currently living and working in Pensacola. As an "indie" author, Ali has been writing for many years as a hobby, and with the assistance of the Affinity team has taken her love of storytelling to a new level.

Ali's characters range from cowgirls and psychics, to a healthy dose of supernatural beings. She has written standalone titles and series. Ali is an avid reader, and her other hobbies include photography, outdoor activities, and watching college sports.

OTHER AFFINITY BOOKS

Unknown Forces by Samantha Hicks
Jennifer Wilson has spent the last seventeen years raising her younger sister after an unfortunate boating accident killed their parents. It hasn't always been easy. Riley Blake hasn't had it easy either. Growing up with an alcoholic father and an absent mother. When tragedy and secrets emerge, Jennifer and Riley must learn to lean on each other. When events conspire to keep them apart, will they trust in the love they share or hide from their feelings forever?

A Window to Love by Annette Mori
Two life events, two paths colliding, two souls destined to meet. Mandie Carter lives an uninspired life. No passion, no romance, and just when she thought things couldn't get worse, life throws her a curve ball. Gail Forrester is barely hanging on. Buried under mountains of debt, only her much in demand architectural designs keep her afloat. They must find a way forward together through what life and destiny

has in store for them. Only then can they hope to step into that window to love.

<u>Free Spirit</u> by Erica Lawson
Priory McAllister has fought off boardroom sharks, handled high-pressure jobs, and thought she'd seen it all. She found her dream home and couldn't wait to move in. Unknown to Priory, two ghosts…Rhee and a mischievous Dylan…have inhabited the house since 1935. They have no intention of leaving. Jacey Ryder, Priory's long-suffering secretary, gets to play referee between her boss and a bossy ghost, as each side try to lay claim to the house. What can she do when an unstoppable force (her boss) meets an immovable object (the ghost) besides hope for a peaceful solution? They are like two peas in a pod—two *angry, stubborn* peas in a pod.

<u>Addicted to You</u> by Erin O'Reilly
Elin Prescot's dream to be a top fashion designer is finally within her reach—then Marissa Banks enters her life. Snared by her first taste of passion, Elin is consumed by desire for more. Her life spirals out of control until she meets Doctor Aimee Sullivan, who understands all too well what Elin is going through. Can Elin let Aimee into her heart? Or will her addiction keep her enthralled with Marissa? This story explores first love, intense passion, manipulation of emotions, and the gentleness of real love and true romance.

<u>At Last</u> by JM Dragon
A perfume company in trouble, leading to a town in peril. Old Loves. Unrequited Loves. New passions. Can the reclusive Gene Desrosiers save her family company and the people she cares for, even though some are not aware of it yet? Will an ultimate sacrifice win the day, or will Grady

end up a ghost town of unfulfilled lives? This love story will warm your heart.

Deuce by Jen Silver
When Jay Reid was in her twenties, she had it all. A professional tennis career, Charlotte, the love of her life and a new baby. Charlotte's research vessel, *RV Caspian*, was lost at sea, leaving Jay to raise their child alone. Rescued by a local fisherman, with no memory of her life before, she lives on the Faroe Islands as Katrin Nielsen. Seeing a beached seal one day triggers her memory. Twenty-three years is a long time. Is the love they once shared strong enough to be rekindled or have too many years passed eroding all hope of a happy ever after?

After Dark by Samantha Hicks
Can a love that starts out in terror be real or last? Meredith Ashcroft disappears on her way to a client meeting. Five months later, art gallery manager Stephanie Edwards is also held and tortured by the same sadistic man. Thrown together trying to overcome their shared ordeal, they find themselves falling in love. Is it true love or just an attachment to each other born out of fear for their lives?

The Book Witch by Annette Mori
What if someone had the power to bring characters from a book to life...should they be allowed to glimpse reality? Imara is that person, a book witch who is convinced of her superiority, especially over book magicians. Join award-winning author, Annette Mori, and the gang from Asset Management, The Organization, and the colorful women in The Book Addict to bring you this delightful, magical romance.

<u>Calling Home</u> by Jen Silver
Sarah Frost, director of the Frost Foundation makes her home at a writers' retreat—The Lodge on the Lake. Galen Thomas, who is taking a break from her vet's practice goes to the island to fill the post of handy person. A revelation of events from forty years earlier, threatens what they now call home. Will the lives and loves of Sarah, Berry, and Galen survive the disturbing past legacy?

<u>Reach of the Heron</u> by Angela Koenig
After an automobile accident takes the lives of her parents and nearly her own, Arkadia O'Malley faces a painful recovery. She also seeks custody of her younger sister, Rini, and contends with Irish law. Arkadia's efforts to reunite with her sister are aided by powerful women from this reality as well as from Elsewhere. Will they find her in time to save her?

<u>From Wind and Water</u> by Laura Kovack
Surrounded by the Lands of Earth, Fire, Water and Wind is the Seventh Kingdom. All but Earth have rulers. A new enemy threatens all Lands and it is imperative to find the last ruler of Earth. Morgayne, ruler in Land of Water and Ventus, ruler of Land of Wind, form a tentative relationship in this quest. Will they allow or deny their feelings in this fantasy adventure?

eBooks, Print, Free eBooks

Visit our website for more publications available online.

www.affinityrainbowpublications.com

Published by Affinity Rainbow Publications
A Division of Affinity eBook Press NZ LTD
Canterbury, New Zealand

Registered Company 2517228